W9-BVE-129

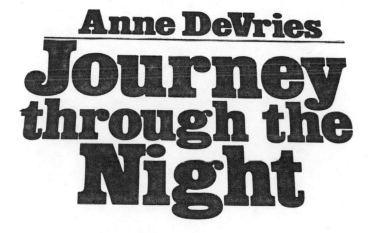

Anne DeVries

Journey through the Night

1. Into the darkness

PAIDEIA PRESS
St. Catharines, Ontario, Canada

First published in Dutch as *Reis door de Nacht,* © G.F. Callenback B.V. of Nijkerk. Translated by Harry der Nederlanden. Illustrations by Anthony Hedrick.

ISBN 0-88815-751-7
Printed in the United States of America.

INTO THE DARKNESS

CHAPTER ONE

When John opened his eyes that sunny Friday morning in May, a thrush was singing by his window. It sang with such persistence and passion that it seemed to be speaking directly to him, and it seemed to have something very important to say. He swung his legs out of bed and, putting his arms on the sill, leaned out of the window. But then the singing thrush dropped from its branch and, screeching loudly, disappeared into the orchard.

"She's not used to people living in the house yet," thought John. He yawned, rubbed his eyes, and looked across the fields. The sun stood just above the pines, but here and there, slender wisps of fog still hung above the ditches that crossed the meadow. The next-door neighbor was already plowing, and steam was rising from the newly turned furrows.

Standing together on the road were three farmers.

One seemed to be doing all the talking. He had quite a story to tell. He pointed to the sky, waved his arms about, and pounded his fist in the palm of his hand. In the quiet morning air, his excited voice carried all the way to John's window, but the words were garbled. "Those farmers get excited over nothing," thought John. "I wonder what happened to get him so steamed up? Maybe his cow had a two-headed calf."

A-a-ah! It sure was beautiful out here in the country. They had moved here from the town of Zeist three days ago, and he was very happy with the move. How busy those three days had been. Everybody had pitched in to put the house in order: he, Mother, Father, Tricia, his fourteen-year-old sister, and Margy, a girl from the neighborhood. They had worked very late last night. At eleven o'clock he had staggered upstairs dead tired, but Mother and Father had still been busy. No wonder they were all still sleeping.

"I know what!" he thought. "I'll surprise them. I'll fix them a nice cup of tea and serve them in bed." Jumping up to go wash himself, he almost tripped over a stack of books. He splashed a little water on himself and hurriedly pulled on his clothes. As he dressed, he studied his new room and planned where to put everything. When the books were in the bookcase and the Frisian landscape was hanging on the wall, the room would look real homey. The corner beside the bed would be a good spot to hang his air rifle; beside it, at a slight angle, he would put his Indonesian spear. And his judo emblem would go right between them. It was his prize possession. He wasn't even sixteen yet, and he had already come a long way in the sport. None of the boys in his class could escape his holds. If only he could keep up his lessons in one of the nearby towns. He had to keep practicing.

But now the tea. Quietly he glided down the stairs into the kitchen and put on the water. Less than fifteen minutes later he entered his parents' bedroom, carrying a tray with four cups of tea and several pieces of rusk.

Mother and Father were still fast asleep, although the sun was almost shining in their eyes. They looked good together. Mother looked like a girl with her soft skin and rosy cheeks, and with his mussed-up hair Father looked very boyish.

John put down his tray and tried to wake them. Because they had worked late, they were hard to rouse. Mother opened her eyes first and looked around as if she were lost. Then she laughed.

"Whew!" she said. "I was in the middle of a dream. What time is it?"

"You have only to listen, your highness, and you'll hear the whistle from the creamery," said John bowing deeply. "Which means that it's exactly 7 o'clock."

He perched on the foot of the bed with his own cup of tea.

"Shouldn't you call Tricia first?" asked Mother.

"She's already sitting in bed drinking her tea," answered John. "She was a lot easier to wake up than you two. I only knocked once and she popped right up. How do you like it? Don't I brew a great cup of tea?"

They praised his tea-brewing skills enthusiastically. "But," added Father, "you didn't put enough sugar in

mine." It was hard to put too much in his tea. He had a sweet tooth.

"What were you dreaming about, Mother?" Father asked. "It must have been some dream! You were hollering, 'No, no, no.' And you almost kicked me out of bed."

Mother laughed. "First tell me, where in the Bible does it say: 'If someone would kill thee, do not defend thyself; for the unrighteous man will kill his own soul.' I woke up with that text in mind. Isn't that strange?"

"Yes, it sure is," said Father. "Particularly because there's no such text in the Bible. 'If someone would kill thee, do not defend thyself!' That would be a text to tickle the pacifists. Johnny boy, that Mother of yours sure wakes up with weighty matters on her mind."

"It must be because I slept so deeply," said Mother, fishing for excuses. "Today we won't have to work so late. We got quite a bit done yesterday. Here's my cup John. Now make yourself scarce."

"I'm going for a walk in the woods," said John. "It's beautiful outside. Just listen to the birds."

"Wait for me," said Father. He jumped out of bed, slid into his slippers, and grabbed his housecoat.

"Surely you're not going out like that?" asked Mother.

"Why not? That's the nice thing about living in the country. You can go out dressed like this without offending anybody." He washed, brushed his teeth, pulled a comb through his hair, and was ready to go.

Together they strolled along the path through the orchard. The pear trees were in full bloom, and the apple trees were beginning to turn pink. Bees buzzed everywhere. John had just let Nemo, their dog, out of the shed; he dashed ahead and then came barreling back and rolled around in the wet grass. Out of sheer joy he snapped at the pantlegs of Father's pajamas.

Father stopped and looked back. John understood; he was just admiring the house that he had designed and built out here in the country. He had reason to be proud. The low white house with its thatched roof lay beautifully concealed between the trees, blending naturally with the landscape and the neighboring farmhouses. John's father was an architect, and the house was the fulfillment of a dream. He had come back to live where he had been born, among the farmers with whom he had grown up. Now he could devote himself completely to his favorite work: designing country homes in the old Saxon style but with modern interiors.

The chill of night still lingered under the dense sprawl of the trees. As they emerged from the orchard, the sun felt wonderfully warm on their skin. At the end of the windbreak that divided the heath from the pasture, they came upon a small lane and stopped again to look over the fields. As Father came from behind the windbreak, his eyebrows lifted.

"Amazing," he muttered. "That's amazing! Look, John. It's Harm Barelds and Fred Bouwman—walking together. They live right next door to each other, but there's a feud between the two families. They haven't talked to each other in fifteen years. And there they come—walking together like the best of friends. I wonder what happened?"

The two farmers slowly drew closer. Each led a couple of cows on a rope. They were deeply engrossed in conversation with each other and glanced up at the sky every so often. They started visibly when they suddenly came face to face with John and his father. Probably because the latter was a strange sight in his housecoat.

"Wha-a-a!" one of them exclaimed. "Who are you? What are you doing here?" He clenched both hands on his walking stick.

"Ha-ha-ha!" laughed Father. "What a friendly welcome,Fred! Don't you know your old classmate anymore—Everett De Boer? We just moved here a few days ago."

"Everett! It is Everett!" cried the other, reaching for Father's hand. "Man, is that you? You've sure changed. And this is your son? He's almost a man already. I took you both for Germans!"

"Go on!" said Father laughing. "You're joking. Germans? Why Germans?"

"Well, why not?" said Harm Barelds while he shook hands with them. "It's not impossible, is it? Now that we're at war."

The laughter died on Father's lips. "At war?" he repeated slowly.

"Yes, haven't you heard?" said Harm. "Didn't you hear all those planes. They passed over in swarms early this morning with the first light. Huge black airplanes heading west. And didn't you hear the explosions? That was our soldiers blowing up the bridges. But it probably won't do much good. The Germans will be here in a couple hours. That's why we're taking our cows home.

You never know what might happen!"

"God almighty!" exclaimed Father. This, more than anything else impressed John. He had never heard Father use words like that before. The winding path must have seemed too long for him. He made a beeline for home, crashing straight ahead through the undergrowth. John followed right at his heels. A brown creature darted away underfoot. "A fox!" thought John. But his mind hardly registered what a rare discovery this was. Panting, they reached the house and burst into the kitchen.

"The radio," gasped Father. He rushed into the living room to turn it on. "You listen for the news, while I go tell Mother what's happening. My boy, my boy, it's terrible! Those miserable traitors! That confounded Hitler!"

Still breathing hard, John sat by the radio. It was the same station where they'd heard the news last night. There hadn't been a black cloud anywhere on the horizon then. Lately the thought of war had almost disappeared from his mind. Hadn't Hitler recently promised again that he would always respect the neutrality of Holland?

The radio hummed and crackled. Then came a voice, clear female tones filled with outrage. The Queen! John quickly turned up the volume so that the voice could be heard all through the house: "I hereby raise a flaming word of protest against this unprecedented violation of all that is right and decent among civilized nations. My government and I will do our duty. You do yours, everywhere and in all circumstances—everyone at his assigned post with the utmost vigilance and with the in-

ner assurance and resolve of a clear conscience . . . ."
While the Queen was still speaking, the others quietly
entered the room.

"She really laid it on the line!" said Father. "They
haven't licked us yet. Just wait and see! Morale is high
among our troops. They'll fight. They'll fight hard!"

Then he jumped to attention as the national anthem
was played on the radio. They sang along. Never before
had John been so moved at the singing of that old, well-
known song. He looked at his mother. She was pale and
had tears in her eyes, but she sang along bravely. As they
sang, John took her hand in his. They wouldn't dare
hurt his mother, he thought. He drew himself up as tall
as he could and felt ready to do brave and dangerous
deeds. He would protect his mother, even if he had to . . . .

"That was beautiful," said Father when the broadcast
was over. The singing had done him a lot of good too.
He didn't look so pale anymore, and he wasn't as tense.
He almost looked happy. Or was he just putting on a
good front?

"Chins up," he said. "Crying and complaining won't
do any good. Let's plan our strategy. What are we going
to do? It's almost 8 o'clock. If the Germans crossed the
border at daybreak, then we can assume that they'll be
here any time. We're only forty kilometers from the
border. The couple thousand troops stationed in this
part of the country will only slow them a little. Our
troops will withdraw to the Yssel Line, maybe even further. If all the children were here, we'd stay put here at
home. There probably won't be much fighting here.
But . . . ."

Yes, but two of the family were in Scheveningen with Aunt Haddie: twelve-year-old Fritz and three-year-old Trudy. Six-year-old Hanneke was in Hillegersberg near Rotterdam with Aunt Jo. They were farmed out to the family for a few days so that they wouldn't be underfoot during the move. Father was supposed to pick them up tomorrow.

"The Yssel Line will hold them back," said Father. "If not, then the Grebbe Line will. It may stop them for only a little while, but it could stop them permanently. Then we would be separated from the others until the end of the war. Or shall we try to reach them now?"

"Yes," said Mother, "I want to go to the children. Let's go right now, Everett, as soon as possible."

"All right," said Father. "That's what we will do. Now, everybody listen, and do exactly what I say! John, get the car ready and check it out to see if everything's in running order. Tricia, you fix some sandwiches. We'll eat in the car. Mother, pack only what's absolutely necessary. I'll help you after I get dressed. We've got to be on the road in half an hour!"

They scattered. John ran to the garage, then came running back for the car keys. He opened the garage doors and started the DKW. Even though he wasn't sixteen yet, he knew how. When he went along on trips, sometimes his father let him drive long stretches.

The car chugged outside. John turned it around and got it ready for loading. He calculated the amount of gas in the tank with a measuring stick (the car didn't have a gauge), and filled it from a jerry can in the garage. Then he checked the tires. When he returned to the house to report that the car was ready, the radio announcer was giving warnings about German planes. Planes over Gorcum; planes over Utrecht; and over Rynsburg. Parachute troops over Wassenaar and Katwyk. Three planes shot down near Arnhem. John went storming upstairs.

"Dad," he shouted, "Dad! They've already shot down three enemy planes. Isn't that great!"

But Father only shoved a heavy suitcase into his hand.

"Put it in the car," he said, "and then come right back! There's more. Put a jerry can of gas in the trunk just in case."

To get at the trunk, John had to climb into the DKW and fold the backrest of the back seat forward. Nemo jumped in behind him and climbed into the front seat, sitting expectantly with his nose to the window, as if to say, "Oh boy, we're going for a ride!" He would be disappointed.

Tricia came out carrying another suitcase and a bag of sandwiches. Mother brought coats and jackets and the strongbox with all their papers and jewelry. Father locked up the house and tossed a portfolio of sketches into the car—his latest project which he couldn't bear to leave behind. Then he snapped a chain on Nemo and jogged away with him to the neighboring farmhouse. Meanwhile, John packed the trunk. He just managed to fit it all in.

"You going to sit in front, Mom?" he asked, and she could tell by his eyes what he hoped the answer would be.

"No," she said. "You sit with your father."

They had no sooner taken their seats than Father was

back again.

"All set?" he asked. "Then, let's go."

They eased out of the yard. How peaceful the house looked. The surrounding apple trees looked like pink bouquets, and the birds chirped and warbled as if celebrating spring. Did they really have to leave all this behind? Was it possible that right now somewhere not far away soldiers were drawing a bead on each other?

"Whoa!" a high-pitched voice shouted, and the car slammed to a stop. A little bow-legged old man stood in the driveway, blocking the way with outstretched arms. His almost toothless mouth broke into a big grin as he approached Father's window. Father cranked it down. The brown juice of chewing tobacco stained the creases in the old man's chin.

"A fine one you turned out to be!" he said, chuckling. "Drop in between eight and nine in the morning, you said. And here I catch you trying to duck out on me . . . . You aren't already running scared from the Germans, are you, Everett?"

"Not running," said Father. "But three of our children aren't home yet, Uncle Gerrit. We can hardly leave them alone at a time like this! Right?" When the old man nodded, Father continued, "Do me a favor and keep an eye on things here. You were going to work for me. We agreed on that, right? We'll come to an agreement on wages later. I'll give you some money now in case you need something. Who knows when we'll see each other again."

But Uncle Gerrit refused to take anything. "It won't be long," he said. "And in a pinch I've got something put aside. You'll be back soon, don't worry. You'll get to your kids, all right; but you won't outrun the Germans. Tonight you'll go to bed a Hollander, and tomorrow you'll wake up a German." He guffawed.

"Have you so little hope, you old cynic?" Father asked, shaking his head sadly.

"Little hope?" echoed the old man. "No, I've got all kinds of hope. Hitler's bubble will burst, as sure as I'm standing here. First he might conquer half the world, but then his bubble will burst. You can't build on oppression and lies. Not as long as there's a God in heaven. It does my heart good to think how he'll cook his own goose. Well, you'd better step on it. They're getting closer. Drive safely and God bless you. Goodbye!"

He shook Father's hand, curtsied comically to the others, and stood waving and smiling as the car drove off down the road.

"That was Gerrit, Grandfather's hired hand," Father explained. "Now he's going to work for us. And you can bet that he'll take good care of our place while we're gone. He's always full of jokes, but you can count on him. He's an optimist with a difference, isn't he? He accepts the fact that we're going to be beaten, but he's already looking forward to ultimate victory. I wouldn't be surprised if he were right."

Then he lapsed into silence and concentrated on the road. He stepped on the gas, and the DKW leaped ahead, pointing south.

CHAPTER TWO

The journey was without incident until they got into the southwestern part of the province. Father coaxed everything out of the DKW that he could, even taking the corners at top speed. John knew that Father was a good driver, but today he really marveled at his skill. Father seemed to blend with the machine and know exactly what it could do.

The roads were almost deserted. Even in the villages that they passed through, there was rarely anyone in sight. The whole country seemed suspended in silence, waiting for whatever was coming.

"Pretty soon we'll have to decide which road we're going to take," said Father. "We could try to cross the Yssel River at Hattem. Or we could . . . ."

"Look! Soldiers!" said John, sliding forward excitedly.

Several hundred meters down the road, on the outskirts of a small village, stood a figure in a grey uniform. Behind him, half concealed in the trees were other soldiers, with rifles ready. The first figure raised and lowered his arms, signaling the car to stop. Father braked and turned down the window.

"Good morning, sergeant," he said. "What can I do for you?"

"Ha! That's a good sound—the voice of a Hollander," said the sergeant with a laugh. "Your name, and where are you headed?"

Father told him. When he explained about the children, the officer nodded sympathetically.

"Can I go on?" asked Father.

"No, I'm sorry, sir, you can't," replied the soldier. "You'll have to come along to the command post and see the lieutenant. It's close by here. I'm sure everything will be all right then. Drive ahead slowly and I'll walk along. How do you figure to reach North Holland?"

"I don't know yet," said Father, shrugging. "Maybe you can tell me the best way to get there."

"I'm afraid not," said the sergeant, looking shocked at the idea. "Strictly against regulations! You know, military secrets and all that . . . ? Beautiful weather, don't you think? Pretty village, isn't it? See that first road to the right? A beautiful drive. Leads right into Friesland and to the Outer Dike. Beautiful sight, that dike. That's something we're not about to blow up. It's our tie to the rest of Holland. To the left, sir. Our command post. Stop here, please."

He grinned and flashed a quick wink as he turned away. Then he walked up to a young lieutenant standing

on the steps of the town hall and saluted. He told the
lieutenant what Father had told him. Father got out of
the car and stood beside him. The lieutenant acted very
nervous. His hand resting on his holster trembled, and
his mouth twitched strangely. Beside the town hall a
number of soldiers were loading weapons onto a truck.
Ahead, at a bend in the road, a machine gun had been
set up. One soldier knelt behind it, while another stood
staring east through a pair of binoculars. In the village
an old farmer and a couple of boys ran down the street
chasing a pig. Otherwise all was quiet.

"It's all right if I go on, isn't it lieutenant?" Father
asked. "We've got to get our kids!"

"I won't stop you. Go ahead."

"Do you think we can still get across the Yssel Bridge,
lieutenant?"

"I doubt it," he answered quietly.

"Thank you. And the best to you and your men."

Quickly Father climbed into the car, shifted into reverse, and turned the car around. As he drove back, the
sergeant stood along the road and pointed the way with
a big grin. Father waved in appreciation.

"A good man," he said. "And he looks a lot more
self-assured than his commanding officer."

"Yes, but *he* isn't responsible for all those other
men," countered Mother. "And that lieutenant looked
so young. Even though he was nervous, he seemed pretty
determined. I'm sure he'll give a good account of
himself when he has to act."

"Okay, okay. I take it back," Father replied with a
laugh. "I won't bad-mouth him anymore. You're

probably right. After all, you're the expert on men in the family."

"You better believe it!" said Mother. "For example, I can tell that the man sitting in front of me right now is rumbling with hunger. Tricia, take out the sandwiches."

They ate while they traveled. Father drove with one hand, except on sharp corners. Then he'd clamp the sandwich in his mouth as he negotiated the turn.

"Now all I need is a slug of tea to wash it down," he said.

"Do you want to stop to drink it?" Mother asked.

"You mean you've got some?"

Mother laughed with satisfaction. "I didn't want to toss out the pot of tea I made for breakfast, so I poured it into a thermos. Here, John, pass this to your father."

"You're a woman after my own heart," said Father.

"Sure, sure," she teased him. "When it concerns your stomach."

John passed the aluminum cup to Father, who took a swallow and handed it back again. John kept the cup in his hands so that Father could take a drink every now and then. The cup burned his fingers. Mother and Tricia drank from the aluminum cup too. The car purred on from village to village.

"It looks like the people here don't even know about the war," thought John. Farmers were working in the fields, children playing in their yards, and a woman was hanging out the wash. John glanced into the back seat. Mother nodded and smiled at him. Tricia yawned and nestled down in her corner of the seat.

"How is your carsickness, Trish?" John asked

teasingly.

"Sssh!" said Father, elbowing him in the ribs.

Fortunately, Tricia hadn't understood. "What did you say?" she asked sleepily.

"Got anymore sandwiches?" he answered. "On second thought, never mind."

"Nothing more for you, buddy," said Father. "Gluttons and fools are made, not born. Let sleeping dogs lie. What you don't know won't hurt you, and all that. Get my meaning?"

John got his meaning all right. On the trip to their new home a few days ago, they'd had to stop every half hour because Tricia had been nauseated. What if that happened now! And he had almost reminded her. Father winked and Mother laughed a little. It sure was cozy in the car. It was almost as if they were out on a pleasure drive.

But in the next village the people were standing around in groups talking excitedly. They eyed the car too suspiciously for this to be a joy ride. Shortly after they turned onto the highway from Meppel to Leeuwarden, they were stopped and surrounded by soldiers, who trained their rifles on the car. They showed their birth certificates and were allowed to pass. But a few kilometers down the road, they were stopped again. An officer approached the car with his pistol aimed right at Father's face.

"This reminds me of my dream," said Mother.

"You and me both," answered Father. "I can't get it out of my mind. It's almost as if it were a warning from heaven. But this guy must be crazy! He's got his finger on the trigger!" Cranking down the window, Father snapped angrily, "Get that stupid thing out of my face. Do we look like enemy soldiers?"

"It's war, sir," said the officer pompously.

"We're well aware of that," said Father. "But that doesn't mean you have the right to endanger my life. Guns have been known to go off accidentally."

The officer was visibly irritated and got even by posing all kinds of nuisance questions. But when he heard that they were on their way to Scheveningen, his attitude underwent a sudden change.

"Scheveningen? Could you do me a favor? My wife is in Scheveningen. Could you stop and say hello for me and tell her I'm all right?"

"We'll see to it," promised Father. "Just give me her address."

At last! On they went to Heereveen. The roads were getting busier, but almost all the traffic was going in the opposite direction. A big car passed them going the other way, and John glimpsed a couple of pale, frightened faces in the window.

"Jews," said Father. "They've got plenty of reason to be scared. They know what's in store for them if Hitler takes over. In Germany they're being murdered or put in concentration camps. But why are they all heading south? Do they expect to get across the Yssel Bridge? Why don't they cross at the Dike?"

A little further on, they were stopped at the same time as a car heading in the opposite direction, and the mystery was solved.

"You trying for the Outer Dike?" asked the driver.

He was Jewish. "I wouldn't. Not a chance! On the other side of Harlingen they're turning everybody back. No one can get through. We're going to Kampen. Even if the bridge is down, there'll be a ferry. There *has* to be a ferry, or some kind of boat. We've *got* to get across! We've just *got* to!"

The last words were a cry of desperation. The car howled as the driver pressed the gas pedal to the floor and roared off.

Father drove on slowly, frowning with concentration.

"Well, we've been forewarned. But let's try it anyway. We won't stay on the highway, but we'll try to reach Wons by the back roads. Wons is right by the Dike. Hand me that map a minute, John."

He pulled over.

"You take down the top. We can use a little fresh air, and then we can also watch for airplanes."

He studied the chart closely and, when John was finished, he said, "Look, we'll follow this road. See it? It will be your job to guide us to the Dike along this road. We're counting on you, Johnny boy. All the road signs have been taken down, and we can't afford to keep stopping."

John seized the map eagerly. He was a good map reader. On biking trips he was always put in charge of the map. Paying close attention to details was the secret, and accurately estimating the distances between intersections by keeping in mind the scale of the map.

During the next hour, the pasture lands of that corner of Friesland flashed by on both sides—green, yellow, and purple pastures. Then, to the left, they saw the steeple of Wons rising above the fields. They planned to pass the town on the north, but suddenly out of the ditch rose several soldiers. They blocked the road. No one was permitted to go on without a pass. Passes were available in Wons at the parsonage.

"Just ask for Captain Van Eick," they advised. "But don't light any matches near him, or he'll explode and we'll be minus a captain," said one of the soldiers laughing. He was going to add something else, but one of his buddies shoved him and motioned them to drive on. When John looked back, the whole squad was wrestling on the shoulder of the road.

"They haven't any idea how serious things really are," said Mother.

"I wonder what they meant about the matches?" mused John.

"I have no idea," said Father. "I guess we'll find out."

They drove into the village. A long row of cars was lined up in front of the parsonage. Father tried to park behind them but ended up blocking the driveway of a neighboring house. On an impulse, he turned up the driveway and parked in the shadow of a huge chestnut behind a row of shrubs.

"There!" he said. "We're not blocking anybody, and we're also hidden from airplanes. Listen, I hear some now."

As Father and John walked to the parsonage, they saw a formation of some twenty large black airplanes several miles distant. They were flying high, above the dike. They swerved and seemed to follow it. The people in the village watched, pointing excitedly.

"Bombers," somebody said.

"No, troop transports," said another.

"Just wait until our fighters get wind of them," said a soldier. "They'll bring them down one by one like a string of dead ducks."

John watched them, hands over his eyes, to see if any fighters would intercept them until the black planes became tiny spots and disappeared on the horizon. Father had disappeared too. But John found him again on the steps of the parsonage. He was just taking a number from a soldier to wait his turn in line. He got number thirteen.

"Oh, oh! Bad luck," said one of the men waiting in line.

"*If* you're superstitious," answered Father. "How come we have to wait so long?"

"Military vehicles have priority," he was told. "You can't go until there is room!"

There was nothing to do but be patient. Father looked over the other men waiting in front of the parsonage. Again there seemed to be many Jews. One of them, an old man, sat on a suitcase and buried his head in hands that trembled violently. Father went over to him and put a hand on his shoulder.

"Are you okay?" he asked gently.

The man looked up and stared at him blankly for several seconds.

"Hunh!" he snorted and sank back into his former position. Father tried to encourage him, but he didn't respond. Finally, he brusquely shook Father's hand from his shoulder. The old man was a picture of despair. John suddenly felt shaky. He walked back to the car. Mother and Tricia had gone for a short walk, but they hadn't dared to go far, and they were back again, dozing in their seats. John told them that they might have to wait quite a while yet, and then he sauntered back to the parsonage.

The sun was blazing directly on the front door, and the waiting people were sweltering in the heat, but nobody dared to leave his place in line. The day seemed to stand still. A couple of soldiers with notebooks walked along the row of cars, taking down their license numbers. Probably for the passes that they'd soon be issued.

When the parsonage door finally opened, it was past 1 o'clock. But after that, it wasn't long before Father's number came up.

"Come on," he said to John.

In one of the rooms of the parsonage, behind a small desk, sat the captain. He was a huge man with a red face. He asked Father where he was going and why.

"He sure talks funny," thought John.

"How-how did you g-get here?" asked the captain.

"By car," Father replied.

"So," said the big man, grinning. "Your car has just been hab-happo-happropriated by the army."

The big word was almost too much for him. Suddenly John realized what was wrong with him. He was drunk. "Some soldier!" thought John. "He's trying to drown his fear in booze." Now John also understood the soldier's wisecrack about the matches.

Father asked for a pass anyway. The captain scribbled a few words on a piece of paper and directed Father to an adjoining room, where another officer filled in the rest of the pass. He had been following the conversation.

"What's your license number?" he asked.

"L31737," Dad answered.

The officer checked a list on his desk. "Your number isn't here," he said softly, casting a sidelong glance at his commanding officer. Quickly he filled in the pass and stamped it. "Now beat it, while you still have the chance," he said.

In the hall, Father grabbed John by the shoulder. "Did we ever luck out!" he wispered. "They didn't see our car because we're parked off the road!"

When they got outside, the other cars were already being driven away. The owners stood by, watching helplessly. By the hedge, the old Jew sat on his suitcase weeping. Beside him stood a white-haired old woman patting his shoulder.

"Look, Dad," said John hoarsely, his throat strangely tight.

"I know! I'd like to help them all," said Father. "But we can't. Our car is too small. It's full. Come on!"

His voice was hard. And he slammed the car door hard. Then he turned the car around and drove back the way they had come. The same group of soldiers stopped them at the intersection, but one glance at the pass was enough.

"Is our captain still in one piece?" asked the comedian of the group.

"Maybe it would be better for you fellows if he weren't," Father said seriously. "What's going to happen when your lives are on the line?"

"Don't worry," said one of the soldiers, "we'll tuck him in bed and tie him down. We've got a great lieutenant. He'll take over."

"We'll stuff him into a cannon and shoot him at the enemy," joked another. "They can have him, with our compliments."

Father drove away shaking his head. Soon they arrived at the Dike. They were let through the check point without delay and were soon driving along the Dike in a long file of military vehicles. By the time they got to Kornwerderzand, Father had moved to the head of the line. There the road was barricaded, except for a narrow opening. A sergeant held out his hand to see their pass.

"Do you expect any fighting here?" asked Father.

"You can count on it," the sergeant replied. "They'll be here tomorrow."

"Let 'em come!" shouted one of the soldiers stroking the barrel of his machine gun. "We'll have 'em for lunch."

"Good luck!" Father shouted back.

"Our boys are in good spirits, aren't they?" he said, pleased. "Even when their officers fail them, their morale is good. One thing is sure: they won't roll over and play dead for the Germans!"

One lane of the highway had been blocked with rock

piles, barrels, and old wrecks to discourage any planes from using it as a landing strip. The other lane stretched on straight ahead of them as far as they could see. It was past 2 o'clock. Father speeded up to over eighty, passing a convoy of supply trucks and other vehicles. In half an hour they had crossed the Outer Dike without having seen a single plane.

As they passed through the province of North Holland, they ate a few more sandwiches and drank the last tea from the thermos. They were stopped a few more times, but they reached the ferry across the North Sea Canal at Velsen about 4 P.M. There an unpleasant surprise awaited them. An officer riding the ferry went from car to car with the same message: "Your car has been appropriated. Report to the command post on Jupiter Street. Three blocks right and then two blocks left. Got that?"

"What on earth do you want with a crummy little wreck like this?" asked Father. "We've got to get to Scheveningen today to find our kids!"

But the officer was unmoved.

"We can use everything," he said. "We've got to move thousands of troops, three blocks right and . . . ."

"I heard you the first time," Father growled.

He drove off the ferry with a dark frown on his face. Everyone was silent. How would they get on without a car? At the third intersection, a military policeman was turning all traffic to the right. But they were stopped at the next intersection to wait for troops to cross. An enormous number of troops seemed to have been concentrated here; they were crossing the intersection in both directions.

"What would they do if you didn't report?" said Mother.

"Never mind," said Father. "I've been thinking. I don't know if I'm doing the right thing, but I'm going to take you all to Scheveningen first. Then I'll turn over the car. Things are never as hopeless as they look. I know this part of the city like the back of my hand. I used to work here. See those blocks of apartments over there? I supervised the work when they were being built . . . . Good! The street is clear. Here we go."

Quickly he turned right and wound through a maze of small streets until they were back on the highway several kilometers further along. They roared on until they passed through Heemstede, where they were stopped again. The road was blocked by a policeman this time, who told them that a short distance ahead several busloads of soldiers had been shot up by fighter planes and that a number of Red Cross ambulances were on the scene. But it would probably be another couple of hours before the road was cleared.

They parked the car and discussed what to do next.

"If we want to reach Scheveningen today, we've got to take some chances," said Father. "John, take a look at the map. If we turn down this side road, I think we can get on a small road that goes through the dunes and joins the highway somewhere close to Bennebroek. Shall we try it? What do you say, Mom?"

"I'm for anything that will get us to Fritz and Trudy and Hanneke," answered Mother.

"All right, here we go." And Father wheeled the car

around to go back to the turnoff. He heaved a deep sigh.

"What's the matter?" asked Mother. "Getting tired?"

"No. Not at all. I was just thinking about dodging that appropriation of our car. It bothers me. I hope they're appropriating cars in The Hague or Scheveningen. That would make me feel a lot better."

"You could turn it in anyway," suggested Mother.

"Good idea! I'll do that."

"Good idea," Father mumbled again a few minutes later. And he drove more cheerfully, turning the car down the side road. In his heart he had already parted with the little DKW.

CHAPTER THREE

The road through the dunes was bumpy and full of twists and turns. So at the first chance, Father took a road leading back to the highway. According to the map, they should have been past the point where the road was blocked. Nevertheless, when he got to the highway, Father stopped and then inched forward carefully, studying the road in both directions. The broad roadway stretched out in front of them deserted. Moments later they were whizzing on their way again.

Coming around a bend in the road, they suddenly came upon the wrecked buses. One lay half in the canal still smoking. A sickening stench filled the air. Father slowed down, but then suddenly speeded up again. John got a glimpse of a dented helmet, scraps of a uniform, the shattered butt of a rifle, and several dark red blotches. And mother cried out in a horrified voice, "Oh, how awful!"

"What's the matter, Mom?" asked Tricia, who was looking out of the opposite window.

But Mother didn't answer.

"Let's get out of here," she said to Father. "The quicker the better."

"What if more fighters come along?" John asked himself. "I suppose we'd better jump out of the car and throw ourselves into the ditch . . . . But they wouldn't shoot at a little passenger car, would they? They could see that it wasn't carrying any soldiers. Mother's white kerchief must be clearly visible from the sky."

Yet John found himself constantly looking up. Father too kept glancing up apprehensively. But the blue dome of sky stretched out in every direction, cloudless and without any trace of danger.

They passed Bennebroek, Hillegom, and Lisse without slowing down, but then they were once again stopped by a squad of soldiers who had dug in beside the road, close to an intersection. The sergeant ordered them to turn back. It was much too dangerous for civilians to be driving on the highway, he said. But after much talking, Father got permission to turn into a side road at the intersection. This road had more cover and offered more protection against an air attack.

"Where does this road go?" Father asked John.

"If we turn left in a few kilometers, we'll end up in . . . ." The name of the town was obliterated by a sharp crease in the map, so John couldn't finish his sentence.

"Can we get back to the highway further on?"

"Oh sure, Dad. There are *plenty* of roads going that way."

"Good," said Father. He shifted his seat a little, took a good hold on the wheel, and stepped on the gas.

"Aren't you tired yet?" asked John.

"I'm not doing too badly," answered Father.

"Okay, Dad. Do you want me to drive for a while?"

Father laughed.

"I thought that's what you were getting at," he said. "Maybe a little later. Not that I don't trust your driving. But under the circumstances, I think I'd better drive, at least for the time being. Then we can go a little faster. And, well, you never know, something could happen."

"What?" asked John. "What could happen? Turn left up ahead, Dad."

They turned onto a narrow gravel road bordered by fields of tulips and potatoes, separated from the road by large hedges. Here and there stood a farmhouse. Several of them had all the shutters closed. Probably because of the bright sun . . . . But there wasn't a soul to be seen—either out in the fields or along the roads.

Just as John was about to comment on how strangely quiet this area seemed to be, something suddenly appeared on the road ahead. Less than fifty meters in front of them a figure broke out of the bushes and stepped out onto the road. He was wearing an unfamiliar uniform covered with green and black blotches; on his head he wore a deep helmet, and in his hands he carried a rifle.

"We're in for it," Father whispered hoarsely. "A German paratrooper. Be calm. Don't show any fear."

The tires screeched as the German lifted his rifle, aiming it at the car. John ducked down. But nothing happened. The car came to a stop a few meters from the soldier, who was beside the car in a couple of strides.

"The dirty buzzard!" John heard his father mutter under his breath.

"Everybody out!" the soldier shouted in German.

The first thing that struck John was how young the German paratrooper was. Sweat ran in rivulets down his face, and he was panting as if he'd been running.

"Why?" demanded Father. "We're on our way to Scheveningen to fetch our kids."

"Everybody out," he repeated, his voice going high and cracking.

He raised his rifle again.

"We'd better obey," said Father turning around. "We don't have any choice. I think he wants the car. Take the bags out too."

Father spoke in a strangely calm voice. John knew that tone. That's how his father always spoke when he was angry. It meant that he was ready to explode but was fighting to stay in control.

John's heart pounded in his temples. He climbed out of the car and held open the door for Mother. But he kept his eyes fixed on Father. Father switched off the engine, climbed out, and then turned around to reach into the car for a suitcase. But the German shoved him aside and said, "Leave it!" He barked as if he were Hitler himself. "I'm in a hurry," he added looking at Mother and Tricia. It sounded almost like an apology. He slid into the car, put his rifle down beside him, tilted back his helmet and wiped the sweat from his forehead.

"Thanks a lot for everything," he said to the four

stranded travelers standing beside the road. He grinned ironically and turned the key to go speeding off. But nothing happened. He must have been familiar with the make of car, for it was made in Germany. His foot found the starter as if by habit and pressed it down, but the engine didn't turn over.

John shot a furtive look at Father. He knew that the car was hard to start when it was hot as it was now. Even Father often had trouble with it. He called it a temperamental old girl. You had to pump the gas a certain way while you pushed the starter. It took a special little trick. But Father didn't seem ready to share the secret. With an outward calm and with a blank, almost stupid look, he watched the German soldier fumbling around. The starter whined and coughed, but the engine wouldn't catch. John suddenly discovered that he was holding his breath.

The paratrooper scowled at them in frustration, checked the dash board once more, wiped the sweat off his forehead, tried the starter one more time and then screamed, "What did you *do* to this thing?" His eyes showed more fear than anger.

Father shrugged. "It's an old car," he said. "It's been acting up all day. I think the spark plugs are dirty."

Father went to the front of the car and lifted the hood. The German leaped from the car and quickly pushed Father aside. Father's expression didn't change, but John saw his jaw tense and knew that he was fighting to restrain himself. But the soldier paid no more attention to Father; he dug around in the tool box under the hood. He selected the largest wrench, and John noticed that his hands were shaking. That made John feel better. Compared to Father, the German was a frightened kid like himself. He had no idea that Father was putting him on. When Father gave him some helpful pointers, the young man seemed to develop a certain amount of trust in him. He smiled at Father and asked, "You a friend of Germany?"

"Yes, sure," said Father nodding vigorously. "A real good friend!"

"The drawings!" he said softly out of the side of his mouth to Mother. Mother moved to the other side of the car, took the portfolio of drawings from the car and handed them to Tricia. Then she took out one of the bags and the money box. The German was working on a spark plug, but he was having trouble with it. It was extremely hot under the hood. Sweat poured from the soldier's face and dripped down on his arms. Suddenly he yanked off his helmet and handed it to Father. Dutifully Father put the helmet down on the front seat of the car.

"Here, try this wrench," he said, handing him the spark plug wrench.

"Hah, just what I need," the soldier said gratefully.

He grabbed it eagerly and handed Father the big wrench he had been using. Now he had the spark plug unscrewed in no time. He grinned his appreciation to Father and bent forward over the engine again. What happened the next moment imprinted itself on John's mind forever.

Father glanced down the road in both directions. Then he raised the large wrench over his head and

brought it down hard on the head of the paratrooper. The man groaned and slumped forward over the radiator. Again Father brought the wrench down like a hammer.

"Stop, Dad! Stop it!" screamed John.

"Shut up!" he barked. John shut his mouth. He saw Mother's face on the other side of the car, staring, as pale as death. She was clutching Tricia's face to her chest.

Father dragged the young soldier off the road and rolled his body into the ditch. He rushed back, looking down the road again both ways. Then he grabbed the rifle and helmet from the front seat and flung them across the ditch into a wheatfield.

"Hurry, get into the car!" he ordered. "John, start 'er up! Don't forget the bags!"

Then he ducked back into the ditch again. When he came back, he was stuffing some papers into his inside pocket. He also slid something into his pants pocket. Then he shoved John over on the seat and tried to start the car. But the engine still refused to catch.

"What now!" he muttered. He jumped back out of the car, lifted the hood, tinkered with something, and then he was back in the car.

"You forgot to put the wire back on a spark plug," he said. "Now it should work."

"I'm sure a dope," said John. He was nothing but a scared, useless kid. But Father—he had acted fearlessly! He wanted to throw his arms around Father and hug him tightly and hold on. The motor chugged obediently as if it had recognized the hand of its master. Father turned the car around, and they sped back the way they had come.

"We'd better not take another chance like that," Father said. "We'd better get out of here!"

He drove in silence for a while. Then he slapped John on the shoulder and shouted cheerfully, "Well, son, we've still got our car!" Suddenly something snapped inside John. Sobbing, he grabbed Father's arm and clung to it. Tricia started to cry too. Father pulled off the road and stopped under a couple of trees.

"Now it's caught up to me too," he said. He threw back his head and took two deep, shaky breaths. Mother produced a handkerchief and perfume. Father grimaced at the perfume, but it quickly cleared his head.

"Whew! In a minute I'll be as good as new," he said sighing. "War takes a bit of getting used to. But we won the first skirmish, right? If they involve civilians, we have the right to fight back, don't we? Total war, said Hitler. Well, that includes us." He laughed. "First the Dutch army, then the German. But we've still got our car. You think that evens the score?"

"What's going to happen to that boy?" Mother asked softly.

"Don't worry about him. He'll be out for a couple of hours and then he'll stagger around holding his head until he's taken prisoner. He isn't armed, so he isn't dangerous. If we see any Dutch soldiers, we'll report it."

"He's not going to die?" asked John, suddenly breathing easier.

"Not from that little tap," said Father. "Those Nazis

have hard heads; they can take a lot. Maybe I should have—but I couldn't make myself bash in his brains. He seemed so young . . . . But now let's not talk about it anymore, okay? Not now, not ever. Is it a deal? John? Tricia? Let's keep it a secret among the four of us. We were on our way to Scheveningen, right? So let's get going or else we're never going to get there."

They traveled back along the same route they had come until they got back on the highway. The soldiers were gone. They drove on to Leiden without interruption. There they were directed through the middle of the city. They were stopped repeatedly. These soldiers seemed less sure of themselves. Their attitude was threatening and suspicious. At one stop, they were forced to unpack all their things before they were allowed to go on. At another check point, the soldier insisted that Father produce proof that he had three more children.

One sergeant, who recognized Father's northern speech, explained that Nazi sympathizers were creating a great deal of distrust. In some places they were said to have sniped at Dutch soldiers. To make it worse, paratroopers had been dropped all around the city and, although many had been disarmed, others were still wandering about. Some of them, it was rumored, were dressed as civilians. They were expected to try to get into the city under cover of darkness.

"They're trying to get to the Queen and government leaders. Better be careful! Our boys are wound up tight. I'd look for a place to stay, if I were you."

But they drove on and reached Voorburg at dusk. All

around them, tall, pale pillars of light began to sway back and forth against the dark sky, and somewhere antiaircraft fire pounded the sky repeatedly. It was scary to be out on the road.

They were berated by an officer for not having their lights on, but when Father turned them on, he swore and hollered, "Turn em off! Mask those lights!"

But they had nothing to mask the lights with. So Mother took one of her blue skirts and tore it in half to cover the headlights.

Suddenly, above them they heard the throb of airplane engines, and a couple of antiaircraft guns began to hammer away. The frightful howl of an air-raid siren suddenly split the night. They scrambled into the shelter of a doorway and heard fragments of ack-ack come hailing down on the roofs and sidewalks. They stayed there a long time before they got permission to go on.

They still had to make their way through the whole city. But the streets were very quiet and, remarkably, they weren't stopped again. They purred north along Java Street past the Peace Palace. Father knew the road like the back of his hand. Finally, with a deep sigh, he pulled up in front of an apartment numbered 85. It was dark like all the others. Not a glimmer of light showed anywhere. But a small shadow darted out of the blackness of the doorway and came running to the car—Fritz. Uncle Herman and Aunt Haddie were right behind him. "You got through! How on earth did you get *through*?"

But there would be time for questions later. Now they had to unload the car as quickly as possible. John put

the top of the car back up and then parked the car in a
safe place. He locked the doors, and before he walked to
the house, he patted it on the hood. "Good girl," he
said. "You got us through."

Then he ran into the house after the others. They
were sitting together in the family room. Heavy curtains
covered the windows to keep any light from filtering
outside. Aunt Haddie was pouring tea, and she began
fixing something hot for them to eat. Trudy was already
asleep in bed because it was past 9 o'clock. It had taken
them over twelve hours to travel a distance that usually
took them only four hours. Fritz was full of stories
about paratroopers that had been falling from the sky
over the sand dunes, and about dogfights between
fighter planes, and about an airplane that had come
dropping out of the sky.

"It was a German, Dad!" he said. "And when it
crashed, it made a cloud of smoke just like a great big
mushroom." His eyes sparkled as if he were describing a
country fair.

"And on the radio they said that we shot down over a
hundred airplanes. We're winning, aren't we, Dad?"

Father smiled and said that he thought Holland had
done pretty well on the first day of the war. The attack
on The Hague had failed. The first planes had appeared
over the city at 4 o'clock that morning to drop
parachute troops. Reinforcements had been dropped all
day long, and the Germans had captured the airports at
Ypenburg and Ockenburg. But they were retaken by
Dutch troops later in the day.

The Moerdike Bridge over the Meuse River was still in

German hands. But that was nothing to worry about, said Uncle Herman, because the French and English were coming and would take care of the German paratroopers. A large English force was crossing the channel and would land on the Dutch coast some time during the night. Uncle Herman and Father got into an argument, then, as Father skeptically shook his head. But Aunt Haddie put an end to the argument by plunking two steaming bowls of food on the table.

"How'd you do that so quickly?" asked Mother in surprise.

"We've been looking out for you all day. Dig in! Eat all you want. There's plenty."

They all bowed their heads, and Father led in prayer. His voice shook a little as he thanked God for protecting them on their eventful journey.

After supper, Father went into town with Uncle Herman in order to find the wife of the officer who had stopped them in Friesland and to deliver his message. Tricia helped her aunt wash the dishes.

"Did your carsickness bother you a lot?" Aunt Haddie asked her.

And then Tricia suddenly realized that she hadn't once thought of being carsick during the whole trip!

CHAPTER FOUR

The next morning, when John woke up and looked out of the window over the golden dunes, the sun was once again shining brightly in a blue, cloudless sky. He checked his watch and saw that it was almost 8 o'clock. His parents must have let him sleep in because he had been so tired last night. Fritz, who was sleeping in the same room, was still off in dreamland. He lay flat on his stomach, one arm dangling beside the bed.

Were those little clouds out there in the south-west—those little white spots on the blue of the sky? There were ten of them—no twenty. They were slowly sinking lower and lower. Something seemed to be hanging underneath each one. A shock traveled through John's body. "Paratroopers!" The word burst from him so loudly that he thought Fritz would surely come shooting out of bed. But Fritz sat up slowly, glanced out of the window, and said, "That's nothing.

There were lots and lots more yesterday." And he lay back down and yawned.

But John jumped into his pants and shoes, and he was dressed. Everyone had gone to bed half dressed in case something should happen during the night. He bounded down the stairs and rushed outside. A group of people had gathered on the sidewalk and were looking up into the sky. Uncle Herman was there too. He was a schoolteacher and was out on Easter vacation. But none of the other men on the street seemed to have gone to work that morning either.

"They're coming down near Ockenburg," said Uncle Herman. "They must want that airport pretty badly. Listen, you can hear the shooting!"

If you listened carefully, sometimes you could hear the distant rattle of machine-gun fire. Occasionally, a gun shot sounded closer by.

"The dunes are full of German soldiers," said a man with a strange squeaky voice. His long, skinny neck jutted out of the collar of the jacket that he had put on over his pajamas. His face showed fear as well as cunning.

"He's got a face like a rabbit," thought John. "All he needs is a couple of floppy ears."

"Who knows how many were dropped during the night," the man continued. "I heard airplanes all night long. Just wait, by sunset the city will be in German hands."

Some of the people began to growl indignantly and cast threatening glances in his direction.

"How come you're not working?" one man asked him. "You're a policeman, aren't you? They could probably use you right now."

"They'll get along all right without me," answered the squeaky voice. "I just hold down a desk. You wouldn't catch me out on the street at a time like this. What good would it do? We're done for anyway!"

"*You'll* be done for, and sooner than you think, if you don't button your lip," said a husky fisherman. "Some cop!" And he spat on the sidewalk right in front of rabbit-face's feet.

The fellow stepped back in fright and hurriedly explained, "All I mean is, what chance do our boys have against Germany's overwhelming military might? They're just outgunned. They could better lay down their arms and . . . ."

"And if you don't shut your trap, I'll lay you out in the street," snarled the fisherman, taking a couple steps toward the man.

Trying to save face, squeaky voice said defensively, "Come now, can't a person express his opinion around here? This is a free country, isn't it?"

"Yes, but no thanks to you," said the fisherman. "We can do without Nazi spies and sympathizers. Beat it! Get out of here before I knock you clear across the street. And don't come back. You got that?"

He gave rabbit-face a push in the chest that almost toppled him. The latter scurried off to his apartment house. On his doorstep he stopped and turned around, but when the fisherman took a step toward him, he quickly opened the door.

"This isn't the last you've heard of me," he wailed. "Just you wait!" The people laughed. A few kids hooted after him. "You dirty spy! You traitor!" Fritz joined in and shouted louder than anyone else, but his uncle called him back.

"That's enough, Fritz."

"Is he really a spy, Uncle?" asked John.

"No, of course not," replied his uncle. "He's just a stubborn know-it-all. But he'd better watch out. Those fishermen are hotheads!"

The fishermen stood together in a group and eyed the man's house suspiciously.

"You can't trust him," one of them warned. "Yesterday he was nosing around on the docks. He wasn't afraid to be out on the street then. A Jew came up to me and offered to pay me fifty thousand guilders if I'd take him and his family to England. And then this same guy tried to stick his nose into our business. We've gotta keep an eye on him."

Strolling down the sunny street, picking his way between the people, came Father.

"Better get inside and comb your hair a little. You look like you came rolling right out of bed," he said to John. "I'll bet you didn't wash yet either. Better shake a leg. We're taking off again in a few minutes—at least, if everybody agrees. Let's go inside."

He had been in town, he told Mother, to find out what was going on. "It's hard to sort out rumor from fact," he continued; "but who should I run into but Captain Van Dyk. You know, honey, Henry Van Dyk—he was in my class in high school? He's here, and he's on General Winkelman's staff. So I got it right from the top. Who'd have better information than him?

"According to Van Dyk, there's hard fighting going on in Rotterdam. Waalhaven airport has been taken by the Germans; huge numbers of paratroopers were dropped there. They're also in the city. Yesterday they seized the stock exchange. They landed on the Meuse River in seaplanes. I think we'd better try to get Hanneke out of there. She's a couple of kilometers outside the city, but I don't know . . . ."

"You think you can get through?" asked Uncle Herman.

"We've got to try," said Father. "Ypenburg has been retaken by our troops and has been cleared of all Germans. So we can go over Ypenburg. Van Dyk told me in confidence, so don't repeat this to anybody, but today reinforcements are being sent to Rotterdam. If *they* can get through, so can we. Besides, if we can reach Delft, I know a road that bypasses Rotterdam, and we'll be there in a jiffy. Come on, John. Hustle! You're going along."

"And me, Dad? What about me?" asked Fritz, who had been hanging on every word. "I'm coming too, aren't I?"

"No, I'm sorry, son; you can't," Father told him. "John can relieve me at the wheel, if necessary. And on the way back, he can take care of Hanneke. But you're too young to help, and we can't risk your life for nothing."

"Aw, please Dad," he begged.

"That's enough, Fritz. You've heard my answer. No whining!"

John was ready in a flash. He stuffed one sandwich

into his mouth and another into his pocket and dashed outside to get the DKW ready. It was still parked in the same place. Cars weren't being appropriated around here. Fritz was leaning against a wall sulking, and he refused to help John put down the top. He didn't wave either, as the others did, when Father and John drove off toward Rotterdam.

Before they left, Father had made a quick study of a map of The Hague. Now he followed a route that skirted the city. Nevertheless, they were stopped twice. But John had their papers ready so that the delays were not long, and soon they came to Ypenburg. It was very still here. The airport was strewn with burnt-out airplanes and plane fragments tossed about willy-nilly or piled in twisted heaps. Most of them appeared to be German. A foul pallor of smoke drifted over the countryside. They drove by without slowing down, following the road to Delft.

There was no other traffic on the road, and the little black car purred along the broad highway all by itself. Somewhere in the distance a pillar of smoke rose skyward, probably from a burning building. Out in a pasture two cows stood pressed against a gate, bellowing mournfully. But all the people seemed to have disappeared. A strange fear enveloped John, as if somewhere an unseen threat lay in wait for them. He looked at Father and saw the tension etched in his face. His eyes scanned the road and the fields, and his jaw was tightly clenched.

"Look! Over there!" he suddenly hissed, nodding to the right.

But John saw nothing.

"Parachutes!"

Then John saw them too. They were scattered over the pastures, white splotches on the green grass, scores of them. So Germans had been dropped here. But when? Yesterday? This morning? They kept a careful eye out in every direction, but nothing moved. Except they themselves.

On they traveled, and soon the church steeples of Delft appeared on the horizon. But ahead of them was something on the road. If he hadn't known better, John would have said that it was a bird. Only it was much larger. As they got closer, they could see that it was an airplane, a German airplane with a gaping hole in the fuselage. It canted over to one side as if it had tried to land on the road and had hit the shoulder. The DKW could just squeeze by under the shadow of one of its monstrous wings.

Soon they were on the outskirts of Delft. But a viaduct that passed under the road had been blown up. The road was blocked. Huge pieces of roadbed and gravel lined the break in the highway.

They drove up onto the pile of rubble hoping to find a way through. Then they stopped and got out.

"It's impossible," said Father, shaking his head. "We've got to go back."

"If we'd push those chunks and rocks back into the hole . . . ," John started to say, when a piercing whistle sounded close by.

An angry voice shouted, "Get away from there! Move! Right now! Or I'll shoot you myself. Are you

guys nuts? What do you think you're doing? Come
here!"

Parallel to the highway but on a lower level ran a
small service road. On it stood an officer flanked by a
couple of soldiers. He was waving a pistol at them and
working himself into a fury.

"Move!" he shouted again, swearing angrily. "Can't
you hear me?"

"Okay, okay," Father shouted back and climbed into
the car. "Come on, John. He's as mad as a hornet. If we
don't hurry, he'll bust a blood vessel before we get
there."

He backed the small car off the rubble and turned it
around to get to the service road. The officer stood
waiting with great impatience.

"What on earth were you guys doing up there?" he
demanded. "Have you lost your marbles? We're in a
war, haven't you heard? You could have been shot to
pieces. Look! There they come again!"

When Father switched off the motor, the air suddenly
throbbed with the sound of airplane engines. A large
formation was approaching from the east. The metal
birds flickered in the sunshine. Antiaircraft fire opened
up, a siren began to scream, and people scuttled across
the street to a nearby bomb shelter. John and his father
hurried after them. The soldiers hustled John into the
shelter. It was very crowded inside. People stood
pressed against one another. A baby cried with long
choking screams. Quickly John squeezed back to the en-
trance, where his father stood talking with the officer,
who had cooled down a little, but he still insisted that

Father was a reckless fool.

"There's not a single road into Rotterdam that's safe," he argued. "You've gotta be nuts. Take my word for it—your kid will be okay. As long as she stays inside, nothing can happen. But on the road you're risking your neck. The best thing you can do is get back to The Hague as fast as you can!"

The rumble in the sky slowly subsided. Then came the all-clear, and everybody pushed outside. Somebody claimed that three of the airplanes had been shot down, but one of the soldiers told him he was all wet. "They're flying a lot higher than yesterday," he explained. "Our shooting has made them cautious. Now they're flying out of range of our antiaircraft guns."

The scolding by the officer seemed to have scared Father a little, for he kept glancing anxiously at the sky as they sped back to The Hague. They made it without incident and drove slowly through the city streets. They weren't in a hurry anymore. As they turned into one street, they saw a large crowd milling about on the sidewalk. Father drove by, then stopped and parked. He and John got out of the car and walked back to see what was going on. The police had apparently raided somebody's house; a man was being led outside in handcuffs. A large black-and-red flag came fluttering down from one of the upstairs windows. It was caught by the mob below, torn into shreds and trampled underfoot. The police struggled with the crowd to keep them away from the man.

"You stinking Nazi!" they shouted. "Hang the filthy traitor!"

Father grabbed John by the arm and pulled him back to the car. They drove through the middle of town. When they came into the neighborhood of the government buildings, bullets suddenly began whistling overhead and ricocheting off the houses. Father jammed on the brakes so hard that John didn't have time to brace himself, and he was flung forward into the windshield.

Father yanked him by the arm. "Bail out! Head for that doorway!"

They dashed up the steps and flattened themselves against the wall. Father pushed John behind him, trying to shield him a little. Shot after shot rang out. A soldier stalked by right in front of them hugging the buildings, his rifle at the ready, looking from side to side. Father coughed. The soldier spun around, but Father quickly raised his hands as the gun barrel was trained on him. The soldier caught himself, laughed nervously and stalked on. Suddenly he fired. The door behind John and his father burst open, and an officer came running out into the street. He hollered at the soldier, who came trotting back.

"What are you shooting at?" asked the officer.

"At that house across the street," said the soldier, pointing. "Somebody shot at us from there, and I just saw somebody at the window."

"Did you see somebody firing from that house?"

"No sir, but a bullet struck the wall right beside me, and some boys said that it came from that house."

"Don't let yourself get stampeded, soldier," the officer barked. "Hustle back to your post and send your sergeant over here. And don't be so trigger-happy!''

"Yes, sir." He saluted and hurried off.

"And you, sir," said the officer, turning to Father, "get home as quick as you can and don't come out unless it's absolutely necessary! It's dangerous out here, as you may have noticed. All those rumors that Nazi sympathizers are sniping at them have thrown my men into a panic!''

"You don't think there's any truth in it?" asked Father.

The officer shrugged. "I haven't had any confirmation." Then he ducked back into the house.

Father and John drove on as fast as they dared. Once they met an armored car speeding through the center of town. On the outskirts of the city, two Germans who had been captured in the dunes were being brought in. They trudged along, with their hands clasped on their necks, and with Dutch rifles prodding them on. They didn't look at all happy.

By the time Father once again parked the DKW by Uncle Herman's house, it was afternoon. Mother came running to the car, looking very worried. But not because she didn't see Hanneke. She had half expected that they wouldn't be able to reach Rotterdam, for the radio had carried reports of heavy fighting around Delft.

She was worried about Fritz, who had disappeared without a trace several hours ago. After Father and John had left without him, he had acted very surly. He had kept teasing his little sister, and he had stomped around the house, grumbling and whining. Mother had finally sent him up to his bedroom for punishment. But when she checked on him fifteen minutes later, the room was empty. And she was sure he hadn't come down the stairs, because Aunt Haddie was working in the hallway, and she hadn't seen him at all.

He must have made his getaway through the window. Mother had talked to the neighbor lady, and she had told Mother that Fritz had suddenly showed up inside her house, so that she had wondered where he had come from all of a sudden. Fritz must have walked through the eavestrough from his window to the neighbor's window and crawled inside.

A little later, he had gone out with Jobie, the neighbor's boy, who was about his age. They had promised to stay within calling distance, but Mother and Tricia and the neighbor lady had searched the whole neighborhood and hadn't found a trace of the two mischief-makers. What should they do now? Call the police?

"No, of course not," said Father making light of the matter. "Those two little tramps can't have gone that far. I bet they found a little friend; and while you're here pulling out your hair, they're in someone's house making castles with building blocks. Just wait and see. At suppertime their bellies will begin to growl, and they'll head for home."

But an hour later, when supper was ready, neither Fritz nor the neighbor boy had shown up. Father and Uncle Herman tried hard to keep everybody cheered up, but it didn't work. Mother ate very little, sighing deeply every so often; Aunt Haddie kept going into the living room to look out the front window. So after supper a search party was organized: Father, Uncle Herman, John, the neighbor, and another neighbor each took a different section of town to search. They returned one by one without having found a trace of the runaways.

Father still tried to joke about it, but John could tell that he was just as disturbed as everybody else. Deep in his eyes there glimmered a shadow of fear. While Father and the neighbor went out to search once more, Uncle Herman went to the police station. John tagged along with his father. There was a choking sensation in his chest that wouldn't go away. Fritz was a good kid, but he never looked before he leaped. He was blind to danger and was willing to try anything. Sometimes it seemed that he was just looking for trouble. When he was learning to swim, one day he dove off the highest diving board. And when he rode his bike, he didn't pay any attention to traffic signs or anything, at least not when there weren't any police around. What could he have gotten into his head this morning?

The dunes!

"I know, Dad! He's gone into the dunes. That's where the paratroopers were landing this morning, and I'll bet he went to watch the fireworks."

They were about to enter the bank when John said this. Father had just finished saying that he was short of cash and that he'd better take a little out of savings because they were going to need some money tomorrow. He was starting to go through the door, but when he heard John's words, he stopped and came back and gave John a gratified look. "Of course! Why didn't I think of that myself!

"But the dunes are off limits for civilians," he went on, thoughtfully. "Anyone going in there would be turned back by our soldiers."

"That wouldn't stop Fritz," said John. "He'd find a way to sneak around them."

"Listen, John," said Father, handing him the bank book. "You go into the bank and see whether I can withdraw money from our savings account through this bank. We're going to the dunes! If those two little rascals went there this morning already, anything could have happened by now. Let's go, Mr. Jacobs!"

Father lunged down the street with long, swift strides, his fear plainly visible now. Jacobs, the neighbor, a short chubby fellow, trotted anxiously behind him. Sighing deeply, John turned and entered the bank. Silently he framed a prayer for his little brother. He was a little ashamed that he hadn't thought of praying earlier. He hoped it wasn't too late.

The bank was crowded with long rows of people who were also withdrawing money, so John had to get in line and wait. Because he was worried about Fritz, the waiting was very nerve-racking; it gave him a king-size bellyache. He had to stand in line a good half hour before he got to the teller, and then he found that it had all been for nothing.

"I'm sorry, sir," said the teller. "You'll have to take this to the bank in Zeist where the money was deposited. We have no way of getting your money."

"But we *can't* go there," said John. "And my

Father's almost out of money!"

"I'm sorry, but I can't help you," said the teller. "Next, please."

As John slunk away from the counter, a voice suddenly asked, "Are you from Zeist?"

It was a friendly looking, round-faced man standing in line just a couple of places behind him.

"Y-yes," responded John in surprise.

"Then wait here for me until I'm finished," he said. "I think I can help you."

John was rather puzzled, and he thought first that the man was joking. But he waited until the man had been helped, and he seemed to be serious.

"Come along," he said. "My wife is from Zeist, you see, and her whole family still lives out there. She's worried sick that something terrible has happened to them all, and she's been doing nothing but weeping since the Germans struck. All you have to do is tell her that everything is all right over there, and I'll give you twenty-five guilders."

"B-but I don't *know* if everything is all right over there," John protested. "We left there almost a week ago."

"That doesn't matter," the man said, grinning. "Just tell her that you're from Zeist and that when you left, everything was quiet and peaceful. That's all I want. She'll believe you; you have an honest face."

The man held John by the arm as he talked, as if he were afraid that he would run off. He steered John down the street to a little shop near the bank. The shop was filled with pots and pans. A doorbell tinkled as

they went in, and the man yelled, "It's okay! It's just me!" John was led through a door in the back of the store into a small living room.

In the middle of several playing children sat a fat lady peeling potatoes. She quickly wiped her face with a handkerchief; her eyes were red from weeping.

"Hello, Mother," cried the man jovially. "Guess what! Was I ever lucky! Who should I run into at the bank but this here boy from your home town. So now you can hear it for yourself what he's got to say. And I've been right all along. You just didn't want to believe me. He says that everything's okay in Zeist. There's been no fighting, not a single bomb has been dropped there, and there's not a German to be seen. Isn't that right, boy?"

"Uh-huh," said John nodding and smiling. When he saw the sorrowful face of the mother surrounded by all those big-eyed children, suddenly it didn't seem so awful to fantasize a little.

"Don't worry," he added. "You wouldn't even guess it was wartime over there."

"Really?" cried the fat lady. "My boy, you don't know what a relief it is to hear that! I've been so worried, I haven't been able to sleep. And when I get upset, my gall bladder starts acting up, and then I just can't stop crying. It's all related, you know. And my husband kept saying, 'Mother, if anything was happening over there, we'd have heard about it over the radio,' but I said, 'What if they're not reporting everything? What if they . . . .' "

She went on and on, and she hugged and kissed her

smallest child and promised the others that Mommy wouldn't cry any more. She almost floated about the room in relief. Meanwhile, the man had slipped his wallet out of his pocket and stuffed twenty-five guilders into John's hand.

"There you go," he whispered, walking John back to the door. "You give those to your father; that will tide him over for awhile. Sometime when he's got more money than he knows what to do with, he can pay me back."

"B-but you don't even know him," said John in surprise. "Don't you want a receipt or something to prove that you lent me the money?"

"Never mind," said the man, clapping John on the shoulder. "We're all brothers, aren't we? I trust you. You did a great job delivering your message. Go on! Put it in your pocket."

He eased John out of the door and into the street.

"You did a great job," he whispered again. "Thanks a lot! She's a good woman, but her nerves are pretty bad."

The wad of money felt good in John's pocket as he strode down the street. He laughed to himself. A nice guy, that shopkeeper, but his wife was no prize. She was sure nothing like *his* mother. Even though Mother was so worried about Fritz, she hadn't cried at all.

Fritz! He broke into a run. When he turned up the street to his uncle's house, he could tell that the boys hadn't been found yet. The whole family was standing outside in front of the house, and several neighbors had joined them. Father and Mr. Jacobs had gone into the dunes a short distance but had been turned back by Dutch soldiers. Uncle Herman hadn't gotten anywhere at all at the police station. Now there was nothing left to do but wait and pray that everything would turn out all right.

John turned over the money to Father and told him how he had gotten it. He told the story as light-heartedly as possible; he had learned a little about cheering up anxious people. And he actually succeeded in bringing a smile to Father's face. But Mother stood staring off into the dunes, pale and intense; she hadn't even heard the story.

"You short of money, Mr. De Boer?" asked one of the neighbors, who had overheard the story. "If you are, I can help you out a little."

"Same here. I can spare a little," offered another. "Just say the word."

A lady from several doors down came outside with a tray full of cups and served tea to the people standing in front of the apartment house. It seemed as if the whole neighborhood had become family.

"I see them!" someone suddenly called down from an upstairs window. "They're behind the dunes now, but I think I saw them a moment ago. Sure enough! Look! There they come. Straight ahead!"

It was the two boys, all right. They came running across the dunes—Fritz out in front, and chubby little Jobie not far behind. They easily slithered underneath the barbed wire that separated the dunes from the road, and then came strolling down the street as if nothing had happened. Apparently they had not yet become aware of the wrong they had done. They were talking and laughing together and examining something that Fritz had in his hand. Fritz saw his parents and began to run toward them. John noticed that he was holding something under his shirt.

"Dad, Dad!" cried Fritz. "Guess what we saw, Dad? They better go into the dunes right away, Dad. Our soldiers . . . ."

"Inside!" said Father, holding back Mother who wanted to gather her lost son into her arms.

"But Dad! Yes, Dad, but . . . ," Fritz sputtered. "Listen, Dad! Please listen, or else it'll be too late. We made a big discovery, didn't we Jobie . . . ? Where's Jobie?"

A short way down the street Jobie was just being turned over his father's knee, and when he was put back on his feet, he howled angrily, "And now I'm not going to tell you about the Germans that we found!"

"Eh? What?" said Father. "Germans? You saw Germans? What's that you've got under your shirt?"

From under Fritz's shirt slid a dark metallic object. Fritz caught it just in time and handed it to Father. It was an unexploded hand grenade.

"It's a bullet, see?" said Fritz. "We had another one, but Jobie lost it. Right Jobie? It's a good one, isn't it Dad? And look, if you screw off this bottom part, it makes a nice ashtray."

"Don't you ever let me catch you messing with one of these again!" Dad barked, horrified. He handed it to one of the men who held out his hands for it.

"Careful!" the man said. "They're mighty touchy;

they can explode at the slightest bump. I'll turn it over to the army. They'll know what to do with it."

"I wanna keep it," wailed Fritz.

"Pipe down, you little brat!" said Father.

And all the anger that had been building up during the long hours of worrying came boiling up. He grabbed Fritz by the back of the shirt and propelled him up the steps.

"Into the house! I'll deal with you there. You ought to be ashamed, causing your mother so much worry! Sneaking off and going into the dunes! You knew you weren't allowed there!"

Blubbering, Fritz struggled back. He had more to tell. "The Germans! But the Germans!" he cried.

Then he told the whole story. He and Jobie had come upon German soldiers a little way beyond the knoll, only a couple of kilometers away. As they were sneaking through the dunes, they had suddenly heard German voices. When they had crawled closer, through the bushes, they came to a hollow where four German soldiers stood talking together and pointing in various directions. They kept looking at a map held by one of them and then pointed some more.

Then they split up, each of them taking a different side of the hollow, almost at the crest of the dunes, and there each of them dug in. They all had small shovels with which they dug deep holes and then crawled inside. One of them picked a spot very close to the two boys who were hidden under some thick shrubbery. He couldn't see them, but they couldn't move either. If they did, maybe he would have shot them. So they had lain there for hours.

Once Jobie had sneezed because he got sand in his nose. Although Jobie muffled the sound, the German had started and grabbed his rifle. For a long time he scanned the area in all directions before he finally settled back in his foxhole. Later, he ate and took a drink from his canteen, the two boys counting every bite and every swallow, for they too were hungry and thirsty.

After he had eaten, the soldier had put a cigarette in his mouth and then patted all his pockets for a box of matches; he didn't have any, so he crawled out of his hole to get a light from one of the other soldiers.

That's when the two boys had seized their chance to get away. Fritz had wanted to take the little shovel that the German had left beside his foxhole, but Jobie had pulled him away. It was such a nice little shovel—for Trudy to play with in the sandbox, or for him when he wanted to make a hut in the woods. And then they had run home as fast as they could. "Isn't that right, Jobie?"

Fritz's story made a deep impression on everyone. Those boys were something else! They had been eye to eye with the enemy! The grown-ups clapped them on the back and laughed, and Mother couldn't wait any longer to clasp her adventurous son in her arms. She shuddered at the thought of what could have happened had the boys been discovered by the Germans. A lady from one of the upstairs apartments brought a couple of tall glasses of lemonade for the boys, and Aunt Haddie bustled about in the kitchen fixing sandwiches.

Father was standing by, thinking things over, when

suddenly he asked Fritz, "What do you think, Fritz. Could you find your way back to the hollow?"

"Sure! Easy," he answered. "Right, Jobie?"

"Sure, easy," echoed Jobie. "You turn that way after you go over the knoll and then down a seashell path and then climb up the dunes by a big rabbit hole and . . . ."

"Come on," said Father. "We're going to the local command post."

"What about my sandwich?" wailed Fritz. "I gotta have my sandwich first 'cause I'm starving."

So the boys marched off with their fathers, each boy munching on a sandwich. Father also took along the hand grenade to turn it in. A quarter of an hour later they passed the house at the head of a column of soldiers. Proud and pleased, the boys marched alongside the officer like conquering heroes. They took huge strides to keep in step with the soldiers, and they stuck out their chests like strutting roosters. When they disappeared into the dunes, Mother had a sudden fit of terror, feeling sure that something terrible was about to happen to her youngest boy. Almost everyone in the block gathered on the sidewalk in front of the house, to wait in hushed anticipation.

The time dragged on, and the people had slowly begun to wander off, when suddenly heavy shooting broke out beyond the large dune called the knoll. Mother grew deathly pale, and John's efforts to ease her mind, by telling her that the officer would see to it that they stayed out of danger, did no good. She didn't really revive until a short while later when she saw Father and the two young adventurers appear between the dunes.

Immediately, she ran out to meet them.

It would be dark soon. Aunt Haddie had already set the table. She had warmed up the meal that Fritz had missed at noon. He ate like a truck driver but kept jumping off his chair to see whether the soldiers were coming back yet. The shooting had stopped, and the battle was over. While they were still eating, someone outside hollered, "Here they come!" The whole family rushed outside, but when Mother got a good look at the approaching column, she quickly pulled Trudy back inside, and Tricia followed her.

The group that slowly trudged out of the dunes was not a pretty parade. A German supported by two Dutch soldiers headed the column; he seemed to have trouble getting one foot ahead of the other. Around his head was a large bandage soaked with blood, and blood was starting to seep down the side of his face. Behind them came two more German prisoners. With the help of two Dutch soldiers, they carried the body of their fourth comrade between them on a stretcher made from rifles. One arm dangled limply, almost dragging on the ground.

Then came the rest of the Dutch soldiers. One had been nicked in the leg and limped along painfully; another had removed his jacket and was cradling one arm with the other to ease the strain on his wounded shoulder. But they were all grinning, and they waved to Fritz and Father. One of them yelled, "We got them, thanks to you!"

The officer stopped by to tell them how things had gone: they had managed to surround the Germans without being seen and had suddenly opened fire. The four Germans had put up a good fight, but when one of them was killed and another badly wounded, the other two had surrendered. Then the officer shook Fritz's hand and told him that he had a lot of courage and would make a great soldier.

Back at the supper table, everyone was quiet except Trudy, who babbled on about her dolls. Everyone else still saw the pale, bloodied face of the one young German and the limp body of the other. He too had a mother who was waiting for him—now in vain. Perhaps she would never even find out where he was buried. What a waste! Why did this young man who might have lived a long, happy life have to be dropped from a plane far from home, only to be shot dead a few hours later? Did war make any sense? Why didn't they live in peace?

Fritz was the first to recover. He began to tell his story all over again and acted as if he had saved the whole country. He wanted to go outside again right after they had finished eating, and when Father told him, No, he acted so disgusted that he almost got the spanking that he had just missed that afternoon. It had been a long, exciting day for him, and he was so tired that a little later he went to bed without being told.

Outside, it was a quiet evening. The sky had been clear of planes for several hours. The crests of the dunes were steeped in red from the setting sun. Close by, between the dunes, a nightingale filled the evening air with the ebb and flow of his vibrato. In the still beauty of the dusk, war seemed impossible.

Everyone stayed outside until it was almost dark. They talked quietly among themselves.

"Tomorrow's Pentecost," somebody observed.

That's right, Pentecost! John had forgotten all about it. Would the war go on over Pentecost? he asked himself. But his naivete lasted only for a moment. It seemed that God's commandments didn't hold during wartime—at least, the soldiers didn't seem to pay any attention to them.

Listen! Uncle Herman had turned on the radio for the news. The enemy had reached Wageningen and Scherpenzeel, blared the radio. There was heavy fighting around Wons. Over a hundred German planes had been shot down that day; early tomorrow morning, a full-scale attack was expected on the Grebbe Line.

CHAPTER FIVE

That night John was awakened by the sound of gun-shots in the street. Bullets whistled by the house, and excited voices shouted at one another. Then followed another flurry of shots. John sat up in bed, listening; he was just about to hop out of bed to peek into the street from behind the blackout curtain, when suddenly a window shattered and tinkled to the floor. Frightened, he dove under the blankets and waited several seconds, his heart racing; then he stuck out a trembling hand to reach for the light cord over his bed. As the light snapped on, the door opened, and Father stepped into the room.

"Everything okay here?"

Father glanced into the room and immediately turned off the light again because the upper right-hand corner of the blackout shade hung in tatters. The light would show outside, and this was strictly against regulations.

But they could see enough by the faint light from the hall to move around safely. Uncle Herman came into the room too and moved the blackout shade aside to look into the street. John wanted to go and look too, but Father held him back.

"Stay behind a wall. You saw how dangerous it can be to stand by a window," he said.

Nothing moved down in the street, but from high overhead came the drone of airplanes. Had their own soldiers perhaps seen a light in someone's window? But then surely they'd have come to the door and given a polite warning!

Fritz slept through the whole ruckus. He hardly even stirred when Father and Uncle Herman moved his bed into another corner of the room, where it would be more protected from stray shots. He thrashed around a bit and muttered, "Hands up, hands up or I'll shoot!" Then he turned over onto his stomach, cradling his head on his arm—his favorite position—and dreamed on. He was still fighting paratroopers. The shooting continued a few more minutes, but it was further down the street. The rest of the night was quiet.

When John woke up the next morning, the sun was shining merrily through the hole in the shade. The window behind it was shattered, and in the bedroom ceiling was a gaping bullet hole. Fritz still had bits of plaster in his hair. He was flabbergasted that everything had happened without his noticing, and he was angry with John for not awakening him. He'd have loved to hear all that shooting.

Out on the street, some of the neighbors were saying

that during the night someone had been signaling German planes from an attic window. Someone in this apartment block or in the one behind it was a traitor. They speculated about who it could be. The name of the man with the rabbit face, Mr. Schram, was mentioned several times, and the talkers eyed his windows suspiciously. His curtains were still drawn, so he must still be asleep.

"No wonder," they said, "he was probably up all night signaling to the planes. The dirty Judas!"

From high overhead came the low roar of airplane engines. The planes were almost out of sight, and they disappeared in the distance. One man claimed that more paratroopers had been dropped in the dunes early that morning. They were now using a different technique because too many had been killed in earlier drops, he said.

Now they let themselves drop from the airplane like a rock until they were just a few hundred meters from the ground before they pulled the ripcord. That way they were almost down before anyone noticed them; but he had seen them anyway from an attic window. They had come down somewhere in the direction of Ockenburg again.

Not fully dressed yet, Fritz mingled with the adults and listened to all the stories open-mouthed, often joining in the conversation as an equal. He had become the neighborhood darling after yesterday's adventure, and he basked in his fame as people clapped him on the shoulder and smiled at him.

To get him to come in for breakfast was almost impossible. John finally had to go outside and fetch him.

But Fritz resisted, and John had to drag him up the steps by his collar, getting a painful kick in the shins for his trouble. Just then, Father came to the door, and his stern look changed the little rebel into an obedient, if surly, young boy.

John stayed outside on the steps a few moments longer while the finishing touches were being put on the breakfast table. He looked out over the tops of the glaring dunes to the deep blue sky above. Today was Pentecost, the day that the Holy Spirit had been poured out. The sun stood beaming in the sky. Overhead, a skylark sang jubilantly, as if the world were steeped in joy. From Uncle Herman's garden wafted the fragrance of blooming violets; and underneath the shattered window, a peony-rose, with dew still on its leaves, opened its tight little buds to the warmth of the sun. Nature took no notice of the war; it followed its regular course undisturbed.

But for the people in Holland, everything was confusion. Not only didn't it look like Pentecost, it didn't even look like Sunday. Nobody was going to church, for the services had been cancelled. And nobody seemed to be thinking about the miracle that the day was supposed to commemorate. All anybody could think about was the war.

But after breakfast, Uncle Herman took out the Bible and read the Pentecost story. After closing the book, he said, "It's hard to remember that the story I just read is much more important than all the war news we've heard and are going to hear. We should follow the example of the birds and the flowers. We shouldn't allow the war to disturb us either. I know, the war can do us great hurt, but we can't let it rob us of our deepest joy. Flowers are being trampled underfoot, and the nesting places of birds are being destroyed, but the others go on blooming and singing. If such creatures can carry on, why can't we?

"Man can cause a lot of fear and confusion, but God is much greater than all men put together, and today He wants to be very close to us. He wants to give us His Holy Spirit, who makes us strong and happy with a happiness that no man can take away. Let's try to remember that today, shall we? Then, in spite of everything, we can still celebrate Pentecost."

Uncle Herman sat down at the organ, then, and played a Pentecost hymn while the rest of the family sang along.

> "Breathe on me, Breath of God;
> Fill me with life anew
> That I may love what Thou dost love
> And do what Thou wouldst do."

While they sang, Fritz was craning his neck to look out the window. He could hardly wait until the song was finished. Out of the dormers of the apartment block behind theirs, soldiers crawled onto the roof. They crouched behind chimneys and other projections. Sighting their rifles as if to shoot, they shouted garbled words to each other. More soldiers took up positions on the street in front of the building. When the whole street had been blocked off, the soldiers moved in to search the apartments.

"They must be looking for the person who signaled to the planes last night," said Fritz.

Suddenly Aunt Haddie came bustling into the living room with an exasperated look on her face. "What are we going to do?" she exclaimed. "I put a pitcher of milk by the back door to keep it cool in the shade, and now I can't even get it. A soldier yelled at me, 'Get back inside!' He pointed his gun at me. It gave me the willies . . . . And now we don't have milk for our coffee!"

"We can drink coffee without milk," said Uncle Herman calmly. "We can even do without coffee."

There was nothing to be done but wait quietly until the search was finished. The soldiers wouldn't even allow anyone to stand by the window to watch. So John took out a book and began reading. Tricia took Trudy into a corner of the living room and kept her occupied with her dolls; Aunt Haddie and Mother washed the dishes and picked up around the house; Uncle Herman and Father were both busy somewhere else. Outside, an occasional shot rang out, and the soldiers did a lot more shouting. They seemed to be having trouble keeping the people indoors.

"Aunt Haddie, your milk is in the kitchen." It was Fritz. He had not been able to resist the challenge of the pitcher of milk. He had tied an umbrella to a stick, and then, lying on his stomach, he had opened the back door just a crack and slowly pulled the little pitcher toward him. In order to get it inside, he had opened the door a little wider and reached out to grab the pitcher. And he had done it all without the soldiers on the roof noticing anything.

Fritz had triumphed again. Aunt Haddie was happy and hurried into the kitchen to make the coffee. To the scolding he got from Father for taking needless risks, the little hero responded with a pitying smile, as if to say, "I guess everybody can't be as brave as I."

Fritz paced through the house like a caged lion. Once he knocked John's book out of his hands; then he dressed up the cat in doll's clothes; and several times he had to be ordered away from the window by the soldiers outside. Fritz was immensely bored. He didn't like to read, and he seldom opened a book. He was much too restless and impatient.

"Dad, can I go to Jobie's house?" he asked.

"Don't ask foolish questions," said Father. "Nobody is allowed outside."

"I bet if I ask the soldier in front of the door, *he'll* let me go," begged Fritz.

"Well, then try it," answered Father impatiently.

So Fritz dragged a footstool to the front door, climbed on it, and opened the little window in the door. The soldier standing in front of the house suddenly saw a boyish little face appear in the window frame like a living portrait.

"Get out of there, kid!" ordered the soldier.

"Hey, listen mister," began Fritz.

"Beat it, I said!" the soldier growled threateningly. "Or I'll give you such a belt on the nose that it'll end up in your ear."

"Don't you know who I am?" asked Fritz trying to stick his head through the little window.

"Yeah, you're a noisy little nuisance. Beat it!"

"Nope. I'm the kid that pointed out those four paratroopers yesterday. Didn't you hear about that? Jobie, my friend, was there too, and I've got to talk to him. It's urgent. He only lives two doors down. Come on, be a sport! Otherwise, I'll never help you again, and you'll have to fight your old war all by yourself. Then you'll be sorry!"

John and Father stood at the apartment door looking into the hall. They elbowed each other and could hardly keep from laughing out loud. That Fritz! The soldier's face suddenly lit up. Fritz's fame seemed to have spread.

"So, that was you, eh?" he said. "Well, come on then. But hurry up. Two doors down? Come on, hurry! Before the sergeant gets back."

With a whoop of triumph, Fritz kicked back the footstool, yanked open the door, and dashed outside.

"Behave! You hear?" Father shouted after him, but Fritz was already gone.

They breathed a sigh of relief. At last he was out of their hair. "I hope he's not a bother over there," muttered Father.

Suddenly there were loud voices in the street. A prisoner was being led out—Mr. Schram, still dressed in his pajamas just like the day before. He was outraged. His little head bobbed from side to side on his long neck, as he protested loudly. He refused to go, so two soldiers pulled him along, while a third prodded him from behind with a rifle. His wife trailed behind for a way, raising a plaintive yammer. Then she was shooed back inside by a soldier.

"That's where a big mouth gets you," said Uncle

Herman. "I'm sure they'll soon find out he's all right. At least, I can't believe . . . ."

"You're just too trusting," interrupted Aunt Haddie.

"Come, come, Haddie," said Uncle, shaking his head. "There's far too much distrust and suspicion these days. Let's not add to it, dear."

The sun shone right into the bay window of the living room. It was getting hot inside, but they weren't allowed to open any windows. Time passed very slowly. Just as Aunt Haddie was pouring coffee, a shot echoed in the street, and immediately shots rang out from every side. On the roof the soldiers huddled fearfully against their chimneys. One lay in the large eavestrough that lined the roof. He was trying to get a look over the edge.

"Everyone down on the floor," ordered Father. "Over here. This is dangerous!"

Another shot cracked, followed by a second volley. This went on for some time. Only Trudy was enjoying the situation; everyone lay sprawled in her corner among her dolls, and she chortled in delight at all the attention she was suddenly getting. But the others were happy when the shooting stopped and they could get up. Aunt Haddie went into the kitchen to prepare dinner. The soldiers slid down the roof and crawled back into the dormers. Those in the street marched away. Mr. Jacobs brought Fritz back home. Fritz was unusually quiet and didn't meet anyone's eyes. He slipped inside and disappeared. Jacobs remained standing at the door as if he wanted to say something.

"Quite some shooting, eh?" he began, with a sheepish grin.

"Yeah," answered Father. "I can't understand it. You suppose someone was stupid enough to snipe at our boys? I just can't believe . . . ."

"Maybe not," said Jacobs. "But somebody did. Only they couldn't have done much harm. You see, they were only shooting with a toy gun."

Then he spilled the whole story. Fritz and Jobie had played downstairs for awhile, and then they had gone up into the attic. They were so quiet up there that Mr. Jacobs had forgotten all about them. Only after the shooting had been going on for some time did he think of the boys again, so he went upstairs to see if they were safe. As he climbed the stairs, he could tell from their voices that they were having a lark up in the attic, so he quietly crept up the ladder.

"Now it's my turn, okay, Jobie?" he heard Fritz say. And then he caught them in the act. They had found an old popgun of Jobie's and a handful of corks. It was a harmless toy, but it made a surprisingly loud noise. One of the boys carefully opened the little window in the attic while the other stuck the barrel of the toy rifle outside and pulled the trigger. A loud bang reverberated over the rooftops, and a little cork sailed through the air. The skittish soldiers, feeling threatened from all sides, thought that they were being sniped at and shot back blindly at the source of the sound. Roof tiles shattered, and a couple of bullets even penetrated into the attic, lodging in the joists. The two little snipers sat gloating behind a big crate, cheering at every shot that struck the roof.

"Those crazy kids!" exclaimed Father. "You

punished them, didn't you?" He was flushed with anger
and looked around the room for Fritz.

"I boxed their ears and dusted off the seat of Jobie's
pants."

"And that's what Fritz is going to get too," promised
Father. "I should have given it to him yesterday!"

He jumped up to get Fritz, but Mother intercepted
him. She knew that even easy-going Father could lose
his temper.

"Remember, Everett, he's only a child!" she said
anxiously. "Children make games of everything, even of
war."

Father told her not to worry, but he carried out his
decision. So Fritz ended up getting the spanking that he
had managed to escape the day before. The rest of the
day he was unusually helpful and obedient. To feel the
hard hand of his father was something Fritz seemed to
need occasionally; it was like a tonic for him.

That afternoon's news reports, which they had waited
for impatiently, said little that they hadn't heard before.
The announcers seemed to be more selective about what
went on the air. The primary message was that the war
was going well. The Grebbe Line was holding and Wons
was being fiercely defended. The Germans had been
stopped at Brabant, and the first French tanks had
arrived at Vught.

But the stories that circulated on the street weren't
nearly as modest. The French had invaded the province
of Brabant and were chasing the Germans back to their
sacred fatherland; Berlin had been bombed and all the
big munition factories reduced to rubble; a huge

English fleet was gathering off the coast to storm the beaches at dusk.

"In a week's time," people were telling each other optimistically, "there won't be a single Kraut in Holland. But the Allies better take a lesson from 1918 and occupy all of Germany. They'd better not stop until they've got Hitler under lock and key!"

Uncle Herman was jubilant at all these glowing reports, but Father didn't believe a word of it. Toward evening he headed into town to see if he could find his friend Captain Van Dyk and discover what was really going on. It was dark when he returned; Mother had checked the street several times already.

"You never know," she said. "The streets just aren't safe anymore."

Trudy and Fritz were already in bed, but John was sitting in the living room. He had only to look at Father's face to know that the news was far from good. Now it was Uncle Herman's turn to shake his head skeptically; but he couldn't dismiss Father's reports so easily, for they were the latest news from headquarters, told to him in confidence by Captain Van Dyk. Even General Winkelman, the Commander in Chief, didn't know much more.

The war wasn't going at all well for Holland. The Grebbe Line seemed unable to stop the Germans. The Dutch had fought fiercely, and thousands of lives had been lost, but the Germans were at the point of breaking through—if they hadn't done so already. The next obstacle that the German army would face was the so-called Water Line, a defensive maneuver which involved the demolition of dikes and the flooding of large tracts of land. But the question was, would the Dutch troops be able to retreat fast enough to put this Water Line between themselves and the Germans?

The base at Wons had fallen; it had not been able to withstand the heavy bombing. Without any air cover or heavy artillery, and with only flimsy earthen dikes to serve as fortifications, it was only a matter of time. So now the Germans were at one end of the Outer Dike; from there they were moving against the Dutch defenses at Kornwerderzand, where they would get a hot reception—they could count on that!

The biggest threat, however, was in the south. The Moerdyk bridges over the Meuse River were still being held by the Germans, and so was the airport at Waalhaven. House-to-house fighting was reported in Dordrecht. Reports had also come into headquarters that armored divisions were moving along the highway to Moerdyk, but the reports were from civilian sources and therefore not entirely reliable.

But, said Father, if the reports were true, and if the Germans succeeded in making connection with the paratroopers holding the bridges, then the war was lost for Holland. Uncle Herman disagreed with him, and they got into a long argument, which John followed attentively, but which finally put him to sleep. It was past 11 o'clock and high time for him to go to bed.

As John undressed in the dark, gloom seemed to settle on him. He had fervently hoped that the Germans would get a good drubbing, that their treacherous attack would blow up in their faces. Wasn't that the way things had always gone in Holland's history? The Dutch had always outfought their enemies. John's teacher was great at telling stories of past wars. Those were the most exciting times in history class. Everybody in class would lean forward in his desk so as not to miss a word. John would fix his eyes on the teacher and his heart would flutter in suspense.

The stories almost made him wish that one of those wonderful wars would happen today, so that he too could be one of the heroes that the history books glorified. In fact, last Friday morning by the windbreak, when he and Father had met those two farmers and had learned that war had been declared, John had been frightened. But at the same time, as he raced through the orchard behind Father, he had thought, "Oh boy! Now we're going to get some real excitement at last!"

Now John was ashamed at the thought. He had already found that war wasn't at all wonderful. It was a horrible disaster! It meant blood and terror and tears. He thought of the young soldiers at Wons who had been so full of jokes and horseplay. Now they could be lying dead by the side of the road or blown to shreds by bombs. There must be thousands of them lying in the forests around the Grebbe Line, near to the zoo that he had visited a few months ago—thousands of young fellows only a few years older than himself. If he had been born a few years earlier, he might have been among them.

And it was Hitler, that absurd little man with the funny mustache and the hair over his forehead, who was to blame. If only he had never been born, then all those soldiers wouldn't have been killed. Then he would be at home in their nice new house with Mother and Father and all his brothers and sisters. By now he would have had his new room all fixed up and his books put away in his bookcase. He would also be commuting back and forth by bike to his new school in town. There was nothing he would like better now than to be able to pedal back and forth to school in peace.

As he crawled into bed beside Fritz, he noticed that he was crying. He was crying with grief and frustration and hatred at that evil fanatic, Adolf Hitler. John could still hear him screaming over the radio, repeating his pretty promises: "We will never violate Holland's neutrality, never!" When he had spoken those words, his troops had already been massed at Holland's borders. The dirty liar!

He had done the same to Denmark and Norway, and before that to Poland and Czechoslovakia. How could anyone have believed him? If that maniac were only dead, then everything would get back to normal. If only he were lying in the woods with a bullet in his head, instead of those young boys. He lets the others do the fighting for him—the coward! Wasn't there anyone in Germany with guts enough to rid the world of that monster? Such a person would surely get a monument. The whole world would hail him as a hero!

If John got the chance, he would be willing. But would he dare? As he thought about it, he began to doubt himself. He was nothing but a worry-wart, a shilly-shally, too irresolute to get anything done. He was always thinking it over, weighing whether it was the right thing to do, while somebody else went ahead and did it.

About a year ago he had gone to Amsterdam with Father and had spent a whole day taking tests. Later, Father had been sent the results. John wasn't really supposed to see the report, but he had read it on the sly one day when he had seen it lying on Father's desk. That's what the tests had said about him: indecisive. That's why Father had encouraged him to take up judo. It was supposed to teach him to be resolute and aggressive. Father had been pleasantly surprised at his progress. He could be quick to act when he had to be. If only he knew that what he was doing was right.

To get rid of scum like Hitler, who was creating havoc throughout the world—that couldn't be wrong. But it was all just fantasy. He would never get the chance. Or would he? If the Germans won the war, maybe Hitler would make his triumphal entry by riding through the streets of Holland's capital, The Hague. He, John De Boer, would be in the crowd with a pistol in his pocket. He'd stand there very innocently as if he didn't have a worry in the world. But his finger would be on the trigger, and when the smiling villain came by, standing up in his shiny limousine . . . . That's how he always rode through the streets, the brazen fool, without a thought of what a perfect target he made. The pistol came leaping out of his pocket, his finger twitched—bang! The Fuehrer pitched over backward, covered with blood. The war was over!

But, of course, it was just a fantasy. He didn't have a pistol, and it would be impossible for him to get one without his father's knowledge. So he had to plan his

ambush differently. He would do it with his bare hands.
Hitler didn't look very strong in his pictures; he looked
like a weakling. John would have to wait until Hitler
had taken a room somewhere—in a fancy hotel or in the
palace. He'd have to be very clever; he would carry a
special message to enable him to get really close.

Flowers! That was it. He'd buy a bunch of beautiful
white lilacs like those he had seen in those fancy flower
shops. In his wallet he had almost seven guilders—that
ought to be enough. Wearing his Sunday suit and
carrying the big bouquet of flowers, he would go to the
place where Hitler was staying.

There would be a guard, no doubt, who would stop
him. But he would say, "I have flowers for the Fuehrer
that I'd like to give him in person—uh, to show my
devotion to him." That was a lie, of course. But to lie
for such a good cause couldn't be wrong. His German
wasn't too bad either. He had had two years of it in
school. The guard marched off to get permission, while
he waited in suspense. But he had to be calm and
resolute, for he knew that what he was about to do was
right—the best deed in the whole world.

The guard was coming back. He smiled and motioned
to John to come along. The Fuehrer was very pleased
that one of the boys in the newly conquered nation was
so devoted to him. It would give him something to brag
about on the radio. Besides, even a coward wasn't
afraid of a boy in short pants. Little did he know!
Steady as a rock, the boy climbed up the stairs; he was
as resolute as . . . well, as whatever is most resolute. He
waited in a large, splendid hall. Then a door opened,

and in came the Fuehrer with his prickly little mustache, his forelock, and his treacherous smirk.

"Heil Hitler," shouted John, raising his arm—that was part of the act, of course. Then, as he held out the flowers to the Fuehrer in his right hand, John grabbed him with his left and threw him with a left hip toss, his best move. Hitler's body flipped through the air, and the head with the slicked-down forelock smashed down on the marble floor with such force that the whole building shook. A fractured skull, obviously. From his scalp a small trickle of blood ran onto the gleaming marble.

Now came the hardest part—to escape. He was in the lion's den, surrounded by enemies. But he couldn't go on. A sudden pressure in his chest threatened to suffocate him; gasping, he sat up straight in bed. His heart was pounding in his throat, and it was a long time before it got back to normal. In the darkness of the room, he could still see the blood running from the cracked scalp. One thing was sure, he could never kill anybody, not even Hitler himself.

Now he was wide awake. It looked like he was going to be unable to sleep all night. He heard Mother and Father and then Uncle Herman and Aunt Haddie coming upstairs, and he hoped that one of them would come into his bedroom a minute. But they didn't. They thought that he was sleeping, of course, and they didn't want to disturb him. With a sigh he swung his legs out of bed and tip-toed across the cold linoleum to the window. He slid behind the blackout curtain and quietly opened the window. Breathing deeply, he took in the cool night air.

The pale sickle of the moon hung above the knoll out in the dunes; the outlines of the other dunes were barely visible in the night. Stars twinkled peacefully, and from far away came the rustling sound of a breeze—or was it the ocean? A small field owl hooted in the meadows. In the distance, tall pillars of light reached into the sky.

The cry of the owl made John think of that morning. The field owl was hunting mice just as it had always done. God's creation carried on as usual. It was so composed, so resolute, so undisturbed. What were Uncle's words again? We should be like that too. We shouldn't let ourselves be troubled either, and we must not let the war rob us of our deepest joy. It was still Pentecost, the celebration of the Holy Spirit, yet in his mind he had killed . . . .

Ashamed, he looked up into the heavens. The stars seemed as if they were laughing at him. He had it coming—such a stupid dreamer! Maybe God was laughing too. "Don't be silly," He was saying. "Don't forget that I'm still here. I rule the nations. All power on earth and in heaven is in my hands. Avenging injustice isn't your business. It's mine. I won't let satan have his way."

Then John recalled that he had forgotten to say his prayers before going to bed. If he had, maybe he wouldn't have had those crazy dreams. So he prayed now, standing by the open window, looking up at the stars.

"Lord," he said, "I want to be calm and strong and resolute. Help me to trust in You. And bring a quick end to the war."

Then John quietly closed the window. And as he groped for his bed in the dark, he was already yawning.

CHAPTER SIX

The next morning John was sitting in the living room with a book on his lap. Uncle Herman had told him that it was a very exciting story, but John couldn't get interested in it. What did he care about the adventures of a cabin boy who lived three hundred years ago? What was happening *today* was much more exciting. Now he was in the middle of a war himself—a war that was bigger and more terrible than any he had ever read about. After three days of fighting, the enemy had overrun most of the country, and it probably wouldn't be long before the rest also fell. What lay in store for them all?

This morning the hours were dragging by for John. Nothing much seemed to be happening. Maybe he was already getting used to the war; this seemed to be true of almost everyone else. People hardly even bothered to look up any more when airplanes passed high overhead and left white trails in a sky that stretched blue and cloudless from horizon to horizon. The wail of air raid sirens was barely successful in getting the people off the streets anymore; they had fled so many times without anything happening. Only if there were policemen or soldiers about, did they run indoors. If they weren't near home, they would seek cover in the house of a stranger, and the first topic of conversation would, of course, be the war. But John wasn't interested in this kind of conversation; it made him none the wiser. All kinds of conflicting stories were circulating. They all had to be taken with a grain of salt.

John wandered outside, book in hand, and sat down on the steps. He leaned back against the wall in a narrow strip of shade that was starting to inch over the steps. The sun had been shining on the brick for hours, so it was very warm against his body. Every day was as beautiful as the one before, as if the weather looked with favor on the German invasion. Had it rained and stormed every day, perhaps the invasion wouldn't be going as smoothly as it was. Why didn't the heavens do something against the savage horde that was seeking to conquer the world? You would think that there would be hailstorms and thunder—dreadful thunder, with lightning lashing the German army. Or, better yet, it should strike German headquarters and kill all the generals, and the leader of the whole pack—Hitler himself.

Or maybe he, John De Boer, could invent a secret weapon more powerful than any other: like a system of mirrors that would concentrate the sun's rays into a beam that could cut through anything. It would slice through bunkers and melt tanks; and with this killer ray

John would put a quick end to the war.

Stupid! Why did he always have to come up with such ridiculous daydreams. Just like that crazy dream he had had last night. It was a good thing that nobody could look into his head. But all there was to do was sit around and wait. No matter how badly he wanted to help, there was nothing he could do. He was confined to a couple of blocks; no one was allowed to go into The Hague. At the bridge into town, soldiers turned back everyone without a pass from the commandant, and that wasn't easy to get.

John shut his book, dropped it on the steps, and strolled down the street. He went to check on the DKW, which was still parked in the same spot. It was locked, and Father had the keys, so John opened the hood and studied the motor a while. He rummaged through the tool box and suddenly he was holding the big wrench in his hand; it sent a jolt through his body, and a vivid picture of Father and the paratrooper came before his eyes.

Had that been only three days ago? It seemed much longer. So much had happened in the meantime! What had happened to the paratrooper? Probably he had been taken prisoner. John remembered the man's face as he had crawled behind the wheel—cruel and contemptuous. "I'll bet he's learned not to treat people so carelessly," thought John.

John examined the wrench, but he didn't see anything on it. He tossed it back into the tool box, slammed down the hood, and patted the car's top as he walked away. "Old faithful," he thought. "And we've still got you with us." A cloud of dust rose from the linen top. The car had picked up a lot of dirt on the trip. He decided to give it a good wash. But as he walked back to the house, he changed his mind. Why should he? What difference would it make—the Germans were going to get it anyway.

Soon he was sitting on the steps again, staring at the barren dunes and the dried clumps of dune grass. Here and there, green shoots were struggling to show themselves. What a contrast to the countryside around their new house! There the orchards were blooming, the grain was turning the dark fields green, the meadows were full of flowers, and beyond them stretched large tracts of forest, where you could explore all day long. He wished that they could go back—that the war was over and that they were back in their new house.

This morning, Father had said that it wouldn't last long anymore. That's what Radio Bremen from Germany had said too. But Uncle Herman almost got angry with Father for believing it so easily and for having so little hope. But John thought that Father was right; he had unquestioning faith in Father. Actually, he was sitting here in Scheveningen on the steps of an old apartment building, waiting for the end—the end of the war, but also the end of freedom. Something seemed to squeeze his chest every time he thought about it. Maybe that was what was making him so gloomy and listless.

He almost envied Fritz. Fritz was enjoying himself. Even before breakfast that morning, the officer who had captured the four paratroopers had showed up and taken Fritz along to the school where he and his men were housed. Now it would take a team of horses to get Fritz away from there. Confined to the school and its grounds, the soldiers looked on the fun-loving, mischievous young boy as a welcome diversion. They put an army cap on his head, strapped one of their belts on him, and stitched a couple stripes on his shirt sleeves. Fritz was more than happy to stay with the soldiers, eating their food and taking puffs on their cigarettes. He had such ready answers to those who tried to tease him that he became a center of attention in the barracks.

Father had looked in on him and had given him permission to stay—if he promised to stop smoking. So Fritz had promised, and a sergeant—the man who had been nicked in the leg during the fight with the four paratroopers—promised to keep an eye on him. Fritz even got to ride about town with the soldiers in the back of a truck.

Once they passed the steps where John was lounging. Two soldiers were sitting in the front of the truck with their rifles ready, and two on the back also had their rifles unslung. In the middle stood Fritz. He threw a salute at his older brother, but then he laughed and thumbed his nose.

Fritz could have fun because he didn't grasp the seriousness of what was happening around him. Everything was just a game to him. At suppertime he didn't even come home. A soldier stopped by to relay Fritz's greetings and to say that he had already had supper with them. So Fritz even had his own valet.

In the afternoon, when John was again sitting on the steps in the cool of the shade, Tricia joined him. She gave him half of the chocolate bar that she had got for helping Aunt Haddie in the kitchen. For a long time she said nothing. But John could tell that she wanted to ask him something. They were close and got along very well. Less than a year separated them, and Tricia trailed John by only one grade in school. They had very few secrets from each other.

"What's the matter, Trish?" asked John, tugging playfully at one of her braids. "Something's been worrying you."

She tried to laugh, but her heart wasn't in it. "Tell me the truth. We're losing the war, aren't we?"

"Huh-huh. At least, I think so," said John. "Dad says we are. Is that what's bothering you?"

"Yes, because then the Germans will come here too, won't they? And what's going to happen then? Do you think they'll burn down the houses and plunder them and beat and kill people?"

Those questions had entered John's mind too, and it had also been worrying him. That's how wars used to be fought: the victors robbed wherever they went, and anyone who resisted them was murdered. Now, however, there were rules for war. But would the Germans observe those rules?

John decided not to mention his fears. "Of course not, Trish! Don't bother your head about that! All the countries have signed an agreement on how wars ought to be fought, and plundering and burning are strictly forbidden. The Germans won't bother anyone who just goes on about his own business."

"What do you think they *will* do?"

"Oh, they're just going to give the orders," John said. "They'll treat us as if our country was part of Germany, I suppose. We'll all have to obey Hitler, and we'll probably have to pay a whole lot of taxes to Germany."

"I hope so!" sighed Tricia, relieved. "I mean, I hope that's *all* that will happen. They won't get much from me. All I've got is sixty-five cents, and I'm going to spend it all on chocolate bars before they get here. Wasn't that last one good?"

The worry was gone from Tricia's face. She jumped up and pulled John over backwards. Sidestepping his hands as he grabbed for her leg, she slipped inside the door laughing.

John's attention was suddenly caught by a crowd of people that was beginning to collect at the end of the street. He got up and sauntered over there to see what was going on. It must be quite something he thought. More and more people were coming from all directions, converging on the same place. He hadn't heard such excited voices all day. Halfway there, he caught what they were saying.

The Queen was gone! She had secretly left the country during the night. One of the men in the neighborhood worked in the palace stables, and he had just come home with the news. He had seen it with his own eyes, he said. They had left in the early hours of the morning.

"I bet they've gone to Zeeland-Flanders," said somebody.

"Or to Indonesia," said another.

"No, to England, of course," argued a third. England was close and she would be safe there for the time being.

In any case, the Queen had fled. She had abandoned the country, the people were saying. And so had the government. All the cabinet ministers had also taken to their heels.

"I'd never have expected that from her!" said one woman. "How could she? She's called the mother of our people—is that acting like a mother?" she asked tearfully.

"What else can you expect from those high hats?" said a man in overalls. "As long as things are easy, as long as there's money to be made, we're one big happy family. But as soon as things get rough, they treat us like a disease! She's just like the rest of those capitalists. They make me sick!"

He turned to leave, but a short man with a flushed face came barging through the crowd and blocked his way, shaking his fist under the man's nose. "What do you know, you big loud-mouth! Who says she's deserted us? Just because she's gone to England doesn't mean she's not our Queen anymore. You think you can do a better job of running the country, loudmouth? This is no time to slander the government! What makes *you* an authority? What makes you think *you* know the best thing to do? What do you say, people?" he said, turning to the crowd. "Is this a time to be second-guessing our government? We've got to stand together! We've got to trust our leaders! We're all in the same boat! We're all brothers, right?"

It was the man with the weepy wife who had given John twenty-five guilders a couple of days before. Several people in the crowd cheered and slapped him on

the back. He grew even more flushed.

"Listen, you think I like it any better than you? Shoot, I could cry like a baby. But what good will it do if we all stand here bawling in the street? I'm sure they did what was right. Come on, three cheers for our Queen and our government! Hip, hip . . . ."

But the cheer that went up in the hot street lacked spirit. Some couldn't cheer because they were weeping. Others stood by with clenched jaws, still trying to digest the bad news. Didn't the Queen's flight mean that everything was hopeless—hopeless and lost?

John raced home, taking the steps in one leap. This was important news! He had to tell everybody. But Mother and Aunt Haddie were out visiting a sick neighbor lady, and they had taken Trudy along. Uncle Herman was sleeping on the sofa, and Tricia was busy in the kitchen.

"Tricia, where's Dad?" John panted.

"I think he's upstairs. At least . . . . What's the matter?" she answered.

"The Queen is gone!" he shouted as he ran up the stairs. He knocked on the bedroom door and shoved it open in the same motion. Father was sitting on the edge of the bed, and he looked up in surprise. Quickly he slid a newspaper over something on the dresser. But as he rose from the bed, the newspaper slid to the floor. And there, before John's eyes, in a strip of sunlight that fell across the dresser, lay a gleaming blue-gray revolver. John stared at it open-mouthed for a few seconds, completely forgetting his message.

"Wow, Dad! Where'd you get that?" he asked, stunned.

"Does that give you such a scare?" asked Father smiling. "Surely you've seen a gun before! Better close the door behind you—too bad it doesn't have a lock. I'd rather you hadn't seen it. But you know how to keep a secret. Right, John?"

"Sure Dad. Of course! But you're not . . . ?"

Father laughed. "No, I'm not going to snipe at the Germans when they come. I'm not crazy, if that's what is worrying you. But it might come in handy sometime; we don't know what the future holds. Anyway, I oiled it and packed it in grease, and I hope it stays that way."

"I didn't know you had one," said John. "Did you take it along from home, or did you buy it here?"

"Neither," said Father. "Can't you guess? Remember that nice young fellow that we met along the road? I took the trouble to disarm him, so he couldn't endanger anyone else. You might call it the spoils of war. He owed it to us for the inconvenience he caused us. Right?"

John laughed and sat down to watch Father reassemble the revolver.

"Dad," he said, suddenly remembering why he had come. "The Queen has run away, and so has the government. At least that's what they're saying out on the street. Do you think it's true?"

"What?" Father looked up in surprise and thought for a moment. "Sure! Of course!" he said. "I should have expected it."

He wrapped the gun in a rag and closed the can of

grease. John saw that his hands shook a little.

"Sure," he said again and heaved a deep sigh. "Of course. She couldn't let herself be captured. . . . But how long will it be before she can come back?"

"They're saying that she took off because she was scared and was only thinking of herself," John told his Father.

"That's just nonsense, John!" said Father disgustedly. "What good would it have done the country if she had stayed and been captured by the Germans? It's a good thing she got away. The Nazis would have loved to get their hands on her. She was the first one they were after. Why do you think they tried to surround The Hague on the first day? You bet I'm glad she's gone! Now she can represent us with the Allies and help plan the liberation. Those street rumors are just so much claptrap, John. We can thank God that the Queen's safe!"

Together they went downstairs to tell Uncle Herman. "I wonder where Dad put the gun?" John wondered. But he forgot about it when they got downstairs for Mother and Aunt Haddie had come home in the meantime and had already told Uncle Herman the news. Big Uncle Herman sat on the sofa and cried.

Suddenly John was afraid; he finally realized how serious things were. Abashed, he stayed by the door and didn't dare to look at Uncle Herman.

"Everything's lost Everett. You were right," Uncle said in a strange, tremulous voice.

"Not everything, Herman," Father said consolingly. "Not everything. The world is bigger than the Netherlands."

After they had their tea, Father and Uncle Herman went outside. In front of every apartment block stood groups of people with strained faces, discussing the disturbing news. Every so often Uncle Herman was stopped by neighbors who wanted to know what he thought. It had been a good thing that Father had encouraged him; now he could in turn encourage others. But Uncle Herman also still hoped that it was only a false rumor.

It wasn't long, however, before he had to give up this last hope. At the end of the block lived a man who worked for the city. He had seen a proclamation issued by General Winkelman that made the news official. He had copied it down, and he now read it aloud to the people: "Her Majesty the Queen and her Ministers have betaken themselves elsewhere in order to ensure full freedom of action for themselves under the present circumstances. I appeal to everyone to maintain a united front in these difficult times. . . . "

There was more, but most people had stopped listening. So it was true! Everyone seemed numbed by it. Many spoke out in bitterness and were unwilling to listen to any justification of the government. They acted like bereaved people who have lost someone very close to them. That evening, the streets were quiet and deserted earlier than usual. The people retreated to their homes to reflect on their grief in private.

John and Fritz lay in bed. The late evening light filtered into the bedroom through the cracks around the blackout shade; the broken window had been patched with a piece of cardboard. Fritz wasn't sleepy, and

he was chattering on and on about all the excitement he
had had during the day.

He talked about the soldiers as though they were his
playmates, ". . . and then Hans—you know, that great
big tall guy—he said 'Don't worry, Fritz. So what if the
Queen's gone? She may be yellow, but we're not. Who
needs her anyway! She'd better stay wherever she is. We
don't want her anymore. When the war's over, we'll get
ourselves a king; they've got more guts than queens!'
Who do you think would be our king, John?"

"Oh, go to sleep," John grumbled. "That Hans is just
a big knucklehead! He doesn't know what he's talking
about. You'll see; tomorrow or the next day he'll be
saying just the opposite."

"He will not! The Queen is yellow. That's why she
ran away. And Dad's yellow too, 'cause he says
we're going to lose the war. Hans says . . . ."

"Button your lip, Fritz."

"No! Why should I? Hans says that everybody who
says we're going to lose ought to be taken down a peg or
two."

"If you don't shut up, Fritz, I'll take *you* down a peg
or two! Dad isn't yellow!"

"He is too!"

"No he isn't! You just don't know. . . . Dad has done
more for the war than all those soldiers that you're so
buddy-buddy with."

"Dad? Go on!" said Fritz skeptically. "When?"

"When we were on our way here. Dad. . . . " John
stopped, shocked at himself. What was he saying? He

had promised Father to keep it a secret. Was it safe to tell Fritz?

"Well? What did he do?" Fritz prompted, his curiosity aroused. He sat up.

"Oh, nothing," said John irritated. "Shut up and go to sleep! And don't let me hear you repeating such stupid stuff again."

"That's not fair!" Fritz muttered. "You know, but you won't tell me. Come on, John! What did Dad do? You can tell me."

"Well," said John. "He spent the whole day behind the wheel. . . . "

"Yeah, and then?"

"And he took us through everything. We were stopped again and again, and they tried to make us go back because it was too dangerous, but Dad didn't give up. Even though he was tired, he kept trying till we got through. Dad was braver than any of us. Don't you ever say that Dad is yellow again!"

There! He'd pulled that out of the fire pretty handily, even if he had to say so himself.

"And it's dumb to be mad at the Queen. She's going to Indonesia, and she's going to raise a big army and come back to chase all the Germans out of the country."

"You figure?" said Fritz. "Neat! And I'll bet we can hold off those Krauts till then. If only they'd let big Hans fight! You should see him. He's strong as a bear! You know what he said? 'I'll take one of those Krauts by the legs and club the rest of them to death with him.' And I'll bet he could too! He's not scared of anything at all!"

"Sure he will," said John. "Sure! Good night Fritz."

"I'm going to be a soldier too," whispered Fritz. "I'll be a general. And when I have a great big army, I'll conquer the whole world. Just wait and see if I don't!"

"Great!" moaned John. "Just what we need—another Hitler."

But that didn't seem to make sense to Fritz. He turned over on his side, sighed once, and fell asleep. A few minutes later, he seemed to wake up again, at least partly, for he mumbled, "What did Dad do, John? What did he . . . . Why don't . . . tell me . . . why not . . . ?"

As John lay listening to the thud-thud of the antiaircraft guns in the distance—near Delft, he guessed—he wondered whether Fritz had really been fooled by his quick-witted maneuver.

CHAPTER SEVEN

Fritz disappeared very early the next morning. He had run off with a sandwich in his hand even before Mother and Father came downstairs. The others sat down to breakfast, and over the radio they once again heard confirmation of the news that the Queen and her government had left the country. A statement from Queen Wilhelmina was read, which indicated that she was in England:

"Our heart goes out to our fellow countrymen at home who will have to endure hard times," the voice crackled into the living room. "But with God's help, the Netherlands will one day recover all of her European territory. We have suffered calamities in the past, and the Netherlands has always risen again. Remember those times. This time, too, we shall rise again."

They all stood up as the national anthem was played.

First no one sang along. Then suddenly Father's rich tenor joined the music. So John joined in too and then everyone else. John watched as a dark blot appeared on the fabric of Mother's dress.

Reports on the course of the war followed. The announcer seemed to be trying to talk life into the people again. Extensive reports were given on the battle around Kornwerderzand, where the enemy had been stopped cold. The powerful guns of the naval vessel Johan Maurits van Nassau had even managed to knock out the artillery of the German troops attacking the Outer Dike. The radio also reported that the German parachute troops around The Hague had all been captured, which they knew already.

The report on the Grebbe Line consisted of a few cliches: the Dutch troops were fighting bravely and the enemy had made small gains at the cost of heavy losses. But Father had learned that the Grebbe positions had probably been abandoned already. The announcer said almost nothing about Moerdyk, but downtown the word was out that Dordrecht had been taken by the Germans. Father thought that this was probably true. This meant that the enemy was just outside Rotterdam.

The people in the neighborhood had not given up hope yet, but the fighting spirit of the first few days was gone. Anyone who still talked about large landings of English troops and the support of the French army was met by skeptical smiles. Among the soldiers, the frenzy of the first few days had yielded to a grim seriousness and an impatience to leave their quarters in the city and finally see some action. They were resolved to defend every square inch with all their might. But Father hoped that they would never see action in the densely populated city.

"That would be disastrous," he said. This started an intense discussion among the men standing around on the sidewalk.

John was happy that he didn't have to hang around to listen to all those discussions, and that there was something else to do. He and Tricia had to run some errands. Door-to-door delivery had stopped, so they had to go and get bread, butter, milk, and vegetables from the store.

"Try to find some tea if you can," said Aunt Haddie. Tea was hard to come by because everyone had begun hoarding and supplies in the stores were dwindling rapidly. Aunt Haddie had very few groceries in the house, and Mother had brought almost nothing. To build up a little stock was going to be very difficult.

John and his sister walked to the shopping district. To get some vegetables, John had to stand in line for over half an hour, and then he couldn't find Tricia. She wasn't at the bakery. Or had she been there already? He'd better check, because Aunt Haddie wouldn't want to be overstocked on bread. So John walked on to the grocer's.

There stood Tricia with her long braids, at the head of the line. She was just putting the tea and the butter into her shopping bag. John joined the tail-end of the line that snaked out of the store onto the sidewalk. Behind him the line grew quickly. Tricia squeezed through the crowd and came out of the store. She opened her bag and proudly showed John the tea she had bought.

"Should I take the fresh vegetables?" she asked him. "You might be here for a long time yet."

"Yeah, okay!" said John.

"Do you two belong together?" asked a store clerk who was passing by.

John nodded despite the poke in the ribs that Tricia dealt him.

"Are you here to buy tea?" the man asked.

"Yes sir," said John. "I'll take one bag, please." He thought that since his order was so small, maybe the man would help him right away. "That would be nice of him," thought John.

But the clerk glowered at him and said angrily, "Then take off, kid! You're getting nothing. What do you take us for? You think you're going to get two and somebody else nothing? We don't help hoarders. Get out!"

A loud laugh went up in the store, and the other people looked at John, adding all kinds of wisecracks. John felt himself blush with embarrassment and didn't know what to say. He would have loved to shove the clerk right through the store window. But Tricia pulled him by the sleeve.

"I've already got two of them anyway," she said to the clerk. "So we don't need your old store!"

"See! I told you!" said the man indignantly.

Laughing, Tricia pulled John down the sidewalk. "When I got here, this store was already crowded. But there's another one on the other side of the street, and it wasn't nearly as busy. So I went there first. Now we've got two bags of tea. Neat, eh?"

"You're more on the ball than I am," said John, grinning at her. It took him some effort, for he had been insulted and shamed by the laughter at the store. But what ought he to have done? Should he have lied? he asked himself. But that wouldn't have been right, would it?

He was still mulling it over when they got to the bakery. Then he put it out of his mind. He was silly to get upset over such a little thing when the whole world was going up in flames, he told himself. Enough of that nit-picking!

"Here, you put everything in your bag and take it home," said Tricia. "I'll wait here for a couple loaves of bread."

"Not a bad sister," thought John. Tricia joined the long line of waiting women. John took the groceries, but before going home he decided to take a look in the bookstore.

When he came out of the bookstore a few minutes later, he noticed that something was going on in front of the bakery. The women waiting in line were raising a fuss because a tall kid of about eighteen of so had pushed into line in front of Tricia. There he stood, smoking a cigarette and defying them to do something about it. He didn't feel like standing in line all the time, he said, and he'd been here earlier but had left to get a pack of cigarettes. He had a right to this spot, he said, elbowing Tricia aside and blowing smoke in her face.

John put down his bag and walked over to the line. He didn't hesitate now. He knew exactly what he should do.

"You don't belong there," said John calmly. "If you want to get some bread, go to the end of the line."

The young tough looked down his nose at John and laughed derisively. John was almost a head shorter than he was.

John grabbed him by the arm, pulling and twisting it at the same time, then he kicked the fellow's feet out from under him. The young tough lay sprawled on the sidewalk. It had happened so fast that he didn't realize what had happened until he was dazedly picking himself up off the ground.

Cursing furiously, he charged at John. But John was waiting for him. At the last moment he stepped aside, grabbed the tall kid by the waist, and using the bully's own momentum, flipped him head over heels onto the sidewalk. Ouch!

This time he didn't get up as quickly. He raised himself very slowly and edged over to sit on the curb. He sat there rubbing his head and eyed John cautiously, while the line of women laughed at him. John was standing by his bag, hands on his hips.

"How about another round?" he asked.

"Go fly a kite!" said the tall kid, almost moaning. He stood up, dusted himself off, rubbed his head once more and leaned back against the bakery. He was at the end of the line. With a shaky hand he lit another cigarette. The first one lay in the gutter. He didn't say another word.

John looked away and tried not to hear the praise of the onlooking women. It only embarrassed him. Besides, anyone who had taken judo could have done it.

His instructor wouldn't have been happy with that last toss. He had been a little too slow; he should have flipped the guy when he was still going full tilt.

"I'll wait for you," he told Tricia. He slid down the wall and sat down beside his bag on the sidewalk, his back against the warm store front. A man who had been standing right in front of John at the grocery store came walking by and grinned at him. John winked back unperturbed. He suddenly noticed that he wasn't at all uptight anymore about the way he had been treated by the clerk. All the anger he had felt at his unjust treatment had been taken out on the tall kid. He'd probably tossed him a little harder than he had to. But now he felt as if the score was even. Anyway, the guy had it coming.

The tall kid was standing almost beside him now and was taking his last few puffs on his cigarette. Tricia came out of the store carrying three loaves of bread. As they walked home together, John suddenly noticed smoke curling up out of the bag containing the potatoes and vegetables. To his astonishment, he found a cigarette butt smoldering in the bottom of the bag.

"That dirty creep!" John fumed and turned back to the store threateningly.

But Tricia only laughed. "Come on, John. Who cares? Let him have his sick little joke. It would have been a lot worse if he'd dropped it in the other bag. You already showed him plenty. Could you teach me some of those throws? You never know when they might come in handy."

"We should see if we can take lessons together somewhere," said John. "That's the only way to learn it

properly. You'd be good at it. You know how to take
the bull by the horns! You're so . . . so . . . resolute."

"Resolute! Me?" laughed Tricia. "Are you kidding?
What about you? The way you handled that lanky
lout!"

Nothing could have pleased John more. He felt himself blush with pleasure.

They had dinner early that day because Father wanted
to go to the bank and make one more try to get some
money from his savings account. He hoped that the
bank wouldn't be as busy during the noon hour. John
had nothing better to do, so he tagged along.

It was almost 1 o'clock when they walked into the
bank, and Father didn't have to wait long to be helped.
But this teller also insisted that he couldn't withdraw
money from an account that hadn't been opened
locally. The man was willing enough, however, and he
sympathized with Father's situation. He even called up
the manager, but it was futile. There was nothing to be
done but go home with their mission unaccomplished.

Just as Father and John were about to leave, the air
raid siren sounded. So they were stuck in the bank. A
man who came running in off the street said that the
radio was broadcasting a steady stream of airplane
sightings. That was hardly news, for when they looked
out the window, they could see for themselves.

A large formation of bombers was flying high over the
city, heading south. They glistened like silver in the
noonday sun. Then the antiaircraft guns began to raise a
clamor. The windows rattled from the reverberations,
and small white clouds, like wads of cotton, appeared in

the air beneath and among the airplanes. But the explosions had no evident effect. The droning aircraft continued unhindered. Again and again, new squadrons followed in the wake of the first and then disappeared behind the same chimney.

"They're all heading for England," said a man watching the planes with fascination. "For London. I wouldn't like to be in *their* shoes."

Nobody answered him. They didn't even look up. They just sat on the benches or leaned against the counter looking dull and hopeless. None of them felt like talking any more about the war.

"The whole city will go up in smoke," the man went on as if hypnotized. His voice grew louder as if he were addressing a large audience: "They're going to level everything! When one bomber leaves off, another one will take over. Imagine what it's going to look like—a city of seven million people! Bodies everywhere . . . everywhere . . . bodies . . . . Look! Another squadron of bombers. It's endless, endless!"

Still nobody answered, although he irritated everybody with the way he was going on. He almost seemed to be enjoying his horrible predictions. John noticed his father staring contemptuously at the man.

"I'll tell you, I'd rather be up in one of those planes than in the streets of London," the man went on undaunted.

"Not me," said Father, as if he were talking to himself.

"Not you?" the man reacted immediately. "Not you? You mean you'd rather be bombed than be the one dropping the bombs? Do you know what it's like to be lying dead under a pile of rubble?"

"No," said Father. "And neither do you. But I do know it's better to *suffer* injustice than to *do* injustice."

"That's not the way I see it," said the other.

"That's what I thought," answered Father. "And that's why you're not one bit better than those Nazis! They couldn't care less about justice either."

"What do you mean!" the man sputtered angrily. "Do you know what you're saying?"

"I know exactly what I'm saying," said Father calmly. "But *you* don't. You're carrying on like a fool! You'd be better off keeping your mouth shut!"

"Hear, hear!" seconded a man from the far corner of the room. The teller motioned to Father and said, "Say, I'm sorry the bank can't help you, but maybe I personally could be of some help . . . ."

Father laughed and grabbed his hand and shook it. "Thanks a lot," he said. "You're a good man. But no thanks. I don't like to borrow money. I'll find some way to make out. Of course, if I run stuck, does the offer stand?"

"Of course," said the other. "I'd be glad to help you out anytime."

They had been waiting for almost an hour, and still the all clear hadn't been given. The talker, who had been silent for quite a while, began to grumble that there hadn't been any planes overhead for a long time, so why couldn't they go? Finally, he opened the door and left. But he was stopped outside by two soldiers who had been standing in a doorway across the street, and they ordered him to go back. He didn't obey right away and started making a speech, but suddenly the soldiers trained their rifles on him and the man spun around and made for the door as if the devil were after him. He came storming into the bank, pale and trembling.

"He's a coward to boot," whispered Father to John. "Have you ever noticed how selfish people often lack courage?"

The wait dragged on. They'd been trapped in the bank for well over an hour now. A shapeless fear settled on John. What was happening outside? Why didn't the all clear come? Had someone simply forgotten?

Finally, a long wail undulated over the rooftops, and everybody crowded outside. Everything looked normal. The sun was shining brightly, children came skipping outdoors to pick up their games where they had left off, and older people hurried along the street in both directions. On the corner of the block, however, a crowd had gathered, and people were pointing. Suddenly, John grabbed Father by the arm and exclaimed, "Look Dad! Look at that! Wow! What is it?"

On the horizon a dark, ominous pillar of smoke billowed into the blue sky. It was narrow at the bottom, and it spread out at the top like a huge plume. The top slowly wafted to the west.

"What is it, Dad. Is it a house burning?"

"A house . . . ?" Father repeated slowly. "No Johnny, my boy. That's not a house . . . . That's a hundred houses. Maybe more. Isn't that in the direction of Delft or Rotterdam?" Father asked hoarsely.

It had to be Rotterdam, said a grizzled old fisherman. Rotterdam had been bombed. "That's got to be a horrible mess over there," he said, shaking his old grey head. It was the same thing that the windbag in the bank had said, but now it sounded much different.

Father and John hurried home. Everybody in the neighborhood was outside. People shouted back and forth to each other in a constant flutter. One man claimed that he had heard the explosions.

A boy standing up on the roof of a three-story building yelled down that he could see flames leaping upward through the smoke.

Mother came hurrying down the street to meet them. John thought that she looked strange—kind of pale and wild-eyed. She clutched Father's arm and rested her head against his shoulder for a moment. Father wrapped his arm about her, but John couldn't hear what they said to each other. They stood together on the apartment steps, staring off into the distance where the cloud of smoke kept billowing up farther and farther. Sometimes a dark column would suddenly come coiling out above the others like the doomsday dragon rising out of the sea.

"And, lo, the smoke of the country went up as the smoke of a furnace." These words kept running through John's mind. That's how Abraham saw the smoke rising above Sodom and Gomorrah, the wicked cities along the Jordan. Was Rotterdam a wicked city too? How could that be? There were all kinds of churches there; the city was full of people who loved God—thousands of them. Lot and his daughters had been saved. They had been led out by angels just before the disaster struck. What about Rotterdam? What about Hanneke? Hanneke!

Fear suddenly clutched John's throat. Now he understood the terror in Mother's eyes. Hillegersberg and Rotterdam were joined just like Scheveningen and The Hague. Hanneke was staying with two aunts who lived on the outskirts of the city, close to the tunnel.

What if the bombers had dropped their bombs there? Maybe the whole city had been hit. And Hanneke . . . little Hanneke . . . ? She was only six years old, had blond curly hair and big blue eyes.

"Will you make me a whistle when we get to our new house, John?" she had asked him just before they moved. He had promised, and Hanneke had given him a big smile. Was that the last time that he would see her? Was she lying in Rotterdam now, blown apart by a bomb?

He found it hard to breathe, and he had to lean against the wall because his legs suddenly felt rubbery. He was afraid to look up at anyone.

Then he slipped inside to turn on the radio. But the radio was already turned on; yet he couldn't get any sound from either of the Dutch stations. How come? Didn't they have the nerve to tell the people what had happened?

"I've got to go and see," thought John. "The car can't get through, but if I walk straight across the fields, I can get there. The pillar of smoke will show me the way. We've got to know if Hanneke is still alive!"

As John went outside, a man rode by on a bicycle. "Rotterdam is completely wiped out!" he shouted. "Not a house is left standing. Bodies are piled everywhere!"

Father vaulted down the steps and dashed out into the street to stop the man. "How do you know?" he demanded. "Did you get an official report?"

"Everybody says so!" answered the man. "What's the matter, don't you believe me? Just look at that smoke! That's no wiener roast!"

"Then what on earth do you think you're doing?" said Father angrily. "You ought to be ashamed of yourself!" But the man jumped back on his bicycle and before he got to the corner he was again proclaiming his awful message. Apparently he liked creating a stir.

Suddenly John saw Mother slump against the doorpost; she was deathly pale and her eyes were closed. He jumped forward, but Father was one step ahead of him and caught her. Together they led her into the living room and put her on the sofa. John ran to fetch a glass of water, and Tricia ran upstairs to fetch the cologne. But when they came back, Mother had revived, and she greeted them with a weak smile.

"What a fuss," she said. "There's nothing wrong with me. I think I just got too upset over that . . . that jackass on the bicycle!"

Then, in spite of everything, the whole family burst out laughing. The word sounded so funny coming from Mother—she never used words like that.

"Well . . . that horrible man!" scolded Mother. "Why did he have to open his big mouth? It was hard enough for me to stay calm without having someone like that come along."

Suddenly Mother was sobbing anyway. And, of course, Tricia joined right in. If that wasn't enough, Trudy came traipsing into the living room just then and added her voice to the chorus. But that was just the medicine Mother needed. She became so busy soothing her two little girls that she forgot all about herself.

"Listen, Mom," said John, "and you too, Dad. We all want to know what happened to Hanneke, right? Well . . . if I leave right now and start walking, I'll be in Rotterdam before midnight. I could get through, couldn't I, Dad? Especially at night. I can be back tomorrow by noon, and then we'll all know if she's okay. And then Mom won't have to worry anymore. Well, what do you say? Should I?"

Mother, of course, wouldn't hear of it. But she squeezed his hand in gratitude. Father thought his plan wasn't half bad.

"Let's wait until tomorrow," he said. "If we still don't know anything tomorrow, I'd like to go with you. Have you heard anything over the radio?" But the radio was mute.

Uncle played with the knobs to no avail. He sent John to the neighbors to see if they were receiving anything. But Mr. Jacobs assured them that nothing had been broadcast for several hours. Maybe the transmitters had been bombed, he suggested.

As John hurried back home, an army truck came down the street. Between the soldiers stood Fritz. He was wearing a helmet and an orange sash, symbolizing loyalty to the House of Orange, the Dutch royal family.

"Hi, John! Yay!" he shouted, as if he didn't have a care in the world. It annoyed John so much that he hardly waved back. "He's so self-centered; all he cares about is having fun," thought John. "He doesn't think about anyone else—but maybe at his age he just doesn't know any better."

Aunt Haddie was pouring tea when John entered the living room and, contrary to everyone's advice, Mother came and sat by the table too.

"That's what you think," said Mother in a cheerful voice. "You all drink tea while I stay on the sofa with a glass of water, eh?" She came up beside John and gave him a quick kiss.

"That's for your plan," she said. And then she whispered in his ear. "Have you prayed for your sister?"

John nodded vigorously and said, "Yes, Mom." In his heart he was saying a constant prayer that Hanneke would be all right. It was the only thing able to set his heart at rest. Now John also understood how Mother managed to make jokes while inside she was filled with concern. They nodded at each other with a penetrating look, and Mother squeezed his hand.

After tea, Father tried to get into The Hague, but he still couldn't get any farther than the bridge. Nobody at the command post in the school knew anything about the burning city. The sky was growing darker and darker as the smoke spread across the horizon. The family watched in silence from the living room window. Aunt Haddie was doing some knitting, but every so often her needles paused. Then she would stare outside and shake her head. Trudy sat on Mother's lap. Even she was affected by the somber silence of the grown-ups, and she sat quietly sucking her thumb. The time dragged by ever so slowly. And the radio remained mute.

At about 5 o'clock, a sudden ruckus in the street sent them scurrying outside. At the intersection a block away, a large, disorderly group of Dutch soldiers were pouring into their street. They were hollering and swearing and shooting their rifles. One staggered down the street as if he were drunk; then he stopped and leaned forward against a wall with his arm over his face and wept, his body shaking.

Father, Uncle Herman, and John ran down the street, but when they got close to the soldiers, they had to duck into a doorway because bullets were whistling by a little too close for comfort. The distraught soldiers were making it dangerous to be out on the street. They seemed beside themselves with fury and frustration.

"Hey!" shouted Father. "Hey! What's the matter with you guys?"

A tall young soldier faced Father and stared at him as if he were about to attack. His clothes were disheveled, and he had lost his cap. He shook his fist at Father. "Capitulate!" he shouted. "Capitulate! A fancy word, eh? You know what it means? It means I don't get to fire a single shot. Five days I've sat here waiting for a chance to let fly at those jackals . . . . Five days! And now I won't get the chance. Now it's over! We've surrendered! Surrendered! You hear me? And we've been sitting here just begging for a chance to fight. Surrendered!"

He swore, emptied his rifle into the air, and heaved it

over the barbed wire into the dunes.

Another soldier sobbed, "My girl was in Rotterdam." His face was streaked with tears. "They've killed her! And I can't even fight back. I want to kill me a Kraut! And I'll do it too! Nobody's going to stop me. Who gives a rip about the brass. Those yellowbellies!"

"You're right!" screamed another. A bloody bandage had slid down his head, exposing an ugly wound. "He's right boys! Let's not surrender. We'll refuse! Let General Winkelman go hang! Who needs a pantywaist general like that? Let the Krauts come! Those swine! We'll show 'em . . . ."

But nobody listened to him, for at that moment another group of soldiers came swarming into the intersection. They dumped a couple of straw bales onto the street and while some of them tore the bales apart and shook the straw loose, others began lighting it. Onto the burning straw went their rifles, belts, knapsacks, and uniforms. They prodded the pile with their bayonets to help the fire along. The enemy wasn't going to get their equipment! They'd rather see it go up in smoke. It looked like a funeral pyre. The stinking black smoke drifted between the houses.

Uncle Herman rebelled at the waste, and he wanted to interfere, but Father stopped him. "Let them get it out of their system," he said. "Just stay out of their way. They're like a bunch of madmen. You can't stop them anyway. In fact, it's probably an order. They've probably been told to destroy anything that might be useful to the enemy."

Together they trudged back toward the house. Here

and there, soldiers expressed their anger to anyone who would listen, and many listeners were deeply moved. Women wept and men stood staring into space, dejected and despairing. Father, who had been prepared for this moment for days, was calmer than anyone else. "Let's not lose hope," Father comforted the neighbors. "It's awful what happened! But it was inevitable. We didn't have a chance against Hitler's military machine. But that doesn't mean that everything's lost! Remember the words of the Queen. We'll get our freedom back, maybe sooner than we think."

"Oh yeah?" said a sneering voice. "Who's big enough to take on Germany?"

"I don't know," answered Father. "But this I *do* know: a regime built on lies and murder cannot last. Even if the German army defeats every other country in the world, Hitler's Reich will still collapse. It will collapse because of its own God-denying principles."

This made John think of old Uncle Gerrit, who had said much the same thing. He too had predicted the course of the war. For a moment a feeling of hope and victory welled up in John's heart. But then he saw the smoke from the burning guns and uniforms, and, beyond that, the red-black smoke that hung on the horizon over Rotterdam like the great doomsday dragon. And John's heart was once again flooded with fear and sorrow.

He was about to follow Father inside when a soldier a little older than the rest, who had been listening to Father, came up the steps behind them and spoke.

"You people from up north?"

"Yes," said Father. "How did you know?"

"I could tell by your accent," the soldier replied, smiling. "Which is also what prompted me to speak to you."

"Come inside," said Father. He disappeared into the living room with the soldier. A few minutes later he called Uncle Herman. After a while longer, the soldier left, looking grateful.

John soon found out what had happened. Father didn't keep many secrets from him. The soldier had wanted a set of civilian clothes. He owned a small farm in the province of Drenthe, and he was afraid that all Dutch soldiers would end up as prisoners of war and would not be free to go home for a long time.

Tonight when it was dark, he would come and pick up the clothes. He promised to send them back after he got home. Before the Germans arrived, he meant to hop on a bicycle and calmly pedal back to his family. Any German soldiers that he might meet would take him for a civilian, and he wouldn't be made a prisoner of war.

While they were talking, the door banged open and in stormed Fritz. The acrid smell of smoke clung to his clothes, and his face was covered with dark smudges. He was beside himself with grief. He threw himself on the floor, crying loudly, and wouldn't listen to anyone. Finally, Tricia managed to calm him down. She always knew how to handle him.

"Where's your cap?" she asked.

"I burnt it!" he sobbed. "And my helmet and my sash too. Those stinking Krauts aren't going to get my stuff!"

Winking at the others, Tricia took him upstairs to help him wash and change his clothes. A little later she was sitting with him in the back yard, her arm around him. They seemed to be having a serious talk.

It seemed to do him good, because when everyone was called in for supper, although he was quiet like everybody else, Fritz's appetite wasn't affected in the slightest. He wanted to sit next to Father, and when Father read the Bible for devotions, he rested his head on Father's arm. After supper, he quickly ran off for a visit with Jobie.

Suddenly a voice blared from the radio, which had stood switched on all day. The announcer read a proclamation from the Commander in Chief, General Winkelman. It confirmed that Rotterdam had been bombed, and it explained that Utrecht had been threatened with the same fate. In order to spare the civilian population and prevent further bloodshed, General Winkelman had given the order to stop fighting, except in Zeeland. He called on the people to remain calm and orderly and to win the respect of the enemy by their dignified behavior.

"We need not blame ourselves," said the voice. "Our people and our troops have conducted themselves with courage and resolution."

"Resolution?" thought John. "Was I resolute too? And can I stay resolute? Why don't they say something about Rotterdam?" If only they knew whether Hanneke was still alive, then it would be easier to be resolute.

"Long live the Queen!" shouted the announcer at the end of his message. As the first notes of the national anthem came from the radio, John hurried out of the room. He didn't feel up to hearing it right now. But he had to anyway. It was also playing out in the street. A loudspeaker had been placed on the balcony of one of the upstairs apartments so that those standing outside could also hear.

A couple of fishermen stood on the sidewalk listening and then moved on with bowed heads. They hadn't sung along either. "Who could?" thought John. "The announcer should have known better. It just didn't seem proper. The anthem was a joyful song to be sung with fluttering flags and parades, orange sashes and the sounds of celebration. Would it ever again be sung like that?" He saw Uncle Herman coming toward him down the hall, but he suddenly felt the need to be alone for a while.

"I'm going for a walk," he told Uncle Herman, and he headed into the dunes. He assumed that they were no longer off-limits. The path was blocked by barbed wire, but when he had put a little distance between himself and the house, he crawled underneath it. He roamed around a bit, following rabbit trails, and then he climbed one of the highest hills.

Stretched out before him lay the whole countryside, brilliant in the rays of the setting sun: first the glaring dunes, then the towers and churches and apartment blocks of The Hague, and beyond, bathed in a blood-red glow, the Peace Palace. But the sky behind the Peace Palace was dark with smoke from the ravaged city of Rotterdam. Over there was the enemy, and the country, now conquered, lay waiting quietly for the enemy to come and occupy her and do with her as he wished.

John sighed and turned around. There lay the sea, broad and dazzling, stretching farther than the eye could see. A golden path traced its way over the water right into the setting sun. That's where the Queen was too. A good thing she hadn't stayed. Indonesia was over there and the West—the Allies, England and France and maybe, he'd heard it said, also America.

Germany hadn't won yet. Even the Netherlands still existed. The Kingdom of the Netherlands had not yet disappeared! As he sat there meditating, John suddenly noticed that he was humming the national anthem.

Singing the words softly to himself, he marched through the dunes, heading for home. An airplane came flying low along the coastline. Suddenly it banked steeply and thundered by close overhead, engines roaring, toward the center of the city. John saw the swastika on its wings and heard the air whistling along the fuselage. A German fighter, a vulture swooping down to look over its prey.

"Keep singing," John said to himself. And now his song echoed through the dunes: "And drive away the tyrant who binds my soul in chains . . . ."

When he got back to the street, almost everyone had disappeared. The fire was still smoldering in the intersection, but the soldiers had gone. Father had just returned from a visit to headquarters, and he told them that an order had come from the Germans to put an immediate end to all destruction.

But he also had more important news, for according to the commandant, only the center of Rotterdam had been hit. If that was true, they didn't have to worry about Hanneke.

"Tomorrow we'll see if we can get through by car to pick her up," said Father. "And the day after tomorrow we'll try to get home, or at least part way."

"Can I go along too this time?" asked Fritz.

"Sure, on the day after tomorrow."

"No, I mean tomorrow," howled Fritz. "Please, Dad? Please!"

"Well, okay," said Father, relenting. "If you go to bed right this minute!"

"Yay!" cheered Fritz, and his eyes shone with anticipation. He kissed everybody goodnight, starting with Father and also ending with him. Then he skipped out of the room. He had already forgotten his grief over the surrender.

Mr. Jacobs stuck his head around the corner of the door. "Here comes Schram," he told them. "You should see him; he's strutting like a rooster. He really thinks he's something!"

Sure enough, marching down the middle of the sidewalk came Schram, nodding at everybody and glowing with pride like a homecoming hero. He was still wearing his pajama top under his jacket.

"I don't trust him," said Aunt Haddie. "You'd think that he would try to get back home without being seen. Just look at him!"

Schram had stopped by a group of people that was standing directly in front of their apartment.

"What did I tell you?" they heard him crow. "If we had surrendered two days earlier, thousands of lives would have been saved. Yes sir, the government was in the wrong hands. And it has been for years. But now we'll see some changes. Yes sir!"

No one answered. They stared at him expressionlessly and said nothing. It finally sank into Schram's narrow head that he too might be better off saying nothing. Grimacing, he doffed his hat, inspected it a moment, and then disappeared indoors.

"Better keep an eye on him," said Jacobs. "Unless I miss my guess, in his mind he's already crossed over to the enemy. He's just the kind of cur that would cozy up to them."

Jacobs still didn't leave. Suddenly he asked Father, "I hear you had quite an adventure on the way over here, Mr. De Boer. Had some trouble with a German, did you?"

John's heart lurched. He saw Father's face go taut, and he felt his eyes move in his direction.

"Pardon me? Trouble with a German? Where did you get that idea?"

"I gather it came from Fritz. He's been telling stories to his playmates," said Jacobs. "It did sound a little far-fetched. He said that the guy tried to commandeer your car and that you fought with him. Did he make it all up?"

"Please do me a favor, Jacobs," Father said, putting on an easy smile, "and don't repeat that nonsense to anyone! I don't know where he got that story. After all, he wasn't even with us on the way down here."

Jacobs laughed. "Oh, Jobie can come up with some of the most fantastic stories too. The other day he came home with the story that he'd seen a whale on the beach. It turned out to be an ordinary codfish. I'd better get going. Don't forget, General Winkelman will be on the radio at 10:15. Well, guten Abend, as our protectors say."

"Protectors?" asked Aunt Haddie quizzically.

"Sure. Isn't that what the Germans have been saying from the first day of the war? They didn't come to conquer us, but to protect us from England and her allies. If only they would protect us from the Nazis! Including the likes of Schram, unless I miss my guess."

When Jacobs was gone, Father just sat there quietly, thinking. He looked back and forth from John to Tricia. Tricia blushed and then burst into tears.

"Did you tell Fritz that nice little story?" Father asked softly.

"Huh, huh," sobbed Tricia, nodding. "This morning in the garden. But I made him promise not to tell anyone else. I just wanted to get his mind off things and make him feel better because he was so sad. But he acted like he knew already. He asked me what you had done on the way down here that was so brave."

"That was my fault," confessed John. "A couple days ago, when we were upstairs in bed, he called you a coward, Dad, and then it slipped out. But I only said . . . ."

"That's enough!" said Father. "I've heard enough. I'm disappointed in both of you. Well, what's done is done—as long as it doesn't go any farther. I'll lay down the law to Fritz tomorrow. But let this be a lesson to you. You've got to learn to keep some things to yourself. I think that's one talent we're going to need in the days ahead."

And that was the end of the matter. Nevertheless, it left a sour taste in John's mouth. John resolved that in the future he'd bite off his tongue rather than spill anything he'd been told to keep to himself.

"You look like you've lost your best friend," said Father. "Cheer up!" When they went into the family room to listen to General Winkelman's speech, Father put one arm around Tricia and the other on John's shoulder. The voice of the general trembled. He stressed that he had had no choice and that the decision to surrender had been extremely painful. He ended his speech by urging his listeners not to lose faith and hope.

This time when the national anthem was played, everybody sang along, including John. And something filled his chest when he felt the squeeze of Father's hand on his shoulder and the touch of Mother's hand as she took his arm. They stood side by side and arm in arm. They had no idea what awaited them or how long it would be before they would be free again. But the faith of which the general had spoken would always be with them. Together they sang the ancient anthem—"the song of resolution," thought John.

> My shield and my defender
> Art Thou, O God, my King . . . .

In Him lay their source of strength, no matter what might happen.

CHAPTER EIGHT

It was early morning and after its four-day rest the car stood idling contentedly in front of the house. Fritz had quickly scrambled into the front seat next to the driver, so John resigned himself to sitting in the back.

As they drove off, John looked back. Mother watched them as they turned the corner. She would very much have liked to go along, for she was impatient to see her youngest child. However, worry about Hanneke had kept Mother awake most of the night, and she had to be ready for the long trip up north tomorrow. So Father had persuaded her to stay home and rest. He was very concerned about Mother.

The city was unusually quiet. Now and then a trolley car passed, virtually empty. Here and there people walked along the street. A troop of unarmed soldiers sat in the sun against a wall, waiting dejectedly. As yet, there wasn't a German to be seen.

The car purred along toward Delft just as it had four days ago. Nothing seemed to have changed. At the Ypenburg airport, the twisted wreckage of shot-up planes was still evident, but the smoke was gone, and a small Dutch trainer stood beside the runway undamaged. The bomber that had crashed on the road was still there too. Finally Fritz got a close-up look at one of the monsters that he had seen so often high overhead, and he shouted in amazement.

As they approached, a line of cars was just winding its way around the plane from the opposite direction, so Father had to stop. A Red Cross ambulance led the way, followed by a long row of cars and other vehicles.

In one of the cars John saw pillows, a bandaged head, and a nurse.

"Wounded from Rotterdam," said Father. "They're probably being brought to The Hague because the hospitals in Rotterdam are full. Or because they've been bombed."

The smoke still hung over the city like a black curtain, but it wasn't as dense and dark as the day before. The fires were still burning. As they drove toward the city, they couldn't take their eyes off it. They passed the viaduct near Delft that had forced them to turn back four days ago. But the hole in the road had been filled. A few cars coming to the rough spot from the other way braked hard and then proceeded very carefully. These cars were also full of the wounded.

A little farther down the road lay another plane smashed against the side of the raised roadbed. Dirt and rocks had been sprayed in all directions, and the wings of the plane had been sheared off. "That's the second one!" cried Fritz. "Look! Over there! Another one! And another! And another! Over there!"

They seemed to be everywhere. When they came within sight of Rotterdam, Fritz had already counted twenty-two German planes that had crashed on or near the road. Some were burnt-out shells, and others were damaged hardly at all. At one place, a large troop transport almost blocked the road. They had to drive under one of its wings to get by. Beyond it, the fields were dotted with parachutes. This area must have been a battleground, for here and there in the fields and in the ditches lay the swollen bodies of cows or horses.

To the right of the road, smoke rose from the ashes of a farmhouse. Fritz bounced up and down on his seat in excitement, and he whooped at every new spectacle as if he were at a football game. The terrible drama that had been acted out here meant nothing to him.

Then they saw the first Germans. Two tanks, a few armored cars, and a long row of trucks were parked on the shoulder of the road. The soldiers were taking a break. One was slumped down on the handlebars of his motorcycle, fast asleep—probably a dispatch-rider who had to be ready to go at a moment's notice. Others lay sleeping in the grass behind the trucks, and one stood by the canal stripped to the waist washing himself.

In the middle of the convoy was the field kitchen. The delicious smell of bouillon filled the air. A man in a white apron hacked away at a bloody piece of meat with a huge knife. Father drove by the parked trucks very slowly. Fritz turned down the window and stuck his head out to get a better look. The soldiers were in a good mood. They laughed at each other and made loud wisecracks. Two of them were wrestling playfully. No wonder! The battle was over. They were the victors!

Two Germans stood on the right shoulder and watched idly as the small DKW slowly drew near. As it passed them, one of the soldiers suddenly jumped forward with outspread arms and yelled, "Boo!" at Fritz, who had stuck out his tongue at them. It gave him such a fright that he tumbled backward with a squeal—right against Father. The car swerved sharply, and John heard the two soldiers roaring with laughter. But Father was angry, and he threatened to give Fritz a good pasting next time he made fun of the Germans.

"Or else I'll drop you off at the side of the road and you can walk back to Scheveningen by yourself," Father told Fritz. "You got that, you little knucklehead?"

"Yes, Dad," he answered in a subdued voice.

"Do as I do. Ignore them! Pretend you don't even see them."

Then Father turned off the highway toward a small village. A narrow country road ran from the village to Hillegersberg, which was a few kilometers north of Rotterdam. Now they had a good view of the burning city. They were shocked to see how much of it was smoking: the whole city still seemed to be on fire.

The narrow road was lined with single homes and farm houses. Many of the yards were crowded with people. As their car neared the city, they met group after group of people carrying suitcases, bedding, and housewares. There were mothers carrying children, and men pushing wheelbarrows, and wagons piled high with personal possessions.

"Refugees," said Father.

He carefully steered around them to give them all the room that they needed. But sometimes the road was so narrow that the people had to stand in the grass to let the car pass. Their faces were pale and drawn, and they stared ahead blindly. They had probably lost everything and had no idea where to go.

"The poor wretches!" said Father. "It'll take a tremendous amount of organization to help all these victims. We can be thankful about how well we got through so far. That is, if Hanneke is okay."

Hanneke! That's right! There was so much to see that John had almost forgotten about her.

As they approached Hillegersberg, suspense once again gripped his stomach. Here, too, smoke was rising from among the houses, but only here and there. John began to recognize some of the places; he had spent a couple vacations at his aunts' house. There was the railroad crossing, flanked by a German soldier on either side. And there was the street with all the stores, but its name had slipped his mind. Here, also, many people were lugging all kinds of things around with them. At one house a woman was being carried inside on a stretcher, and in a group of children playing on the sidewalk, one was wearing a white bandage around his head.

Why didn't Father drive faster? It seemed as if they were hardly moving, but the speedometer pointed at 50.

Ahead was the street where the two aunts lived. But someone was blocking the way. The man scowled as

Father tooted the horn impatiently. Ahead lay the block of houses that had been on their minds so much during the last few days. There was the door. Except for a few boards and pieces of cardboard nailed over the windows, the house was undamaged.

Father stopped the car with a squeal and jumped out at the same time. The front door of the house burst open as if they had been expected and out came Aunt Jo looking very pleased. Her expression immediately put their minds at ease. Out from behind her came Aunt Corrie and then Hanneke—little Hanneke dressed in her little blue dress.

She came skipping down the steps and leapt into Father's arms. She pressed her face against Father's, first on one side and then on the other. She was crazy about her Father and overjoyed to see him again. John and Fritz each got a quick kiss, and then she hurried back to Father's arms. Father barely got a chance to greet the two aunts.

Inside the house, Hanneke crawled up on Father's lap and began telling him about all the things that she had seen: the airplanes and the bombs and the neat little house that Aunt Corrie had built under the stairs; how she had sat there with Aunt Jo when the big noise came and how Aunt Jo had held her real tight; how they had prayed, and how God had sent all the airplanes away: "Get away all you airplanes, you mayn't make such a big noise!"

After a while, however, Aunt Jo was able to persuade her to take Fritz into the back yard to look at the parakeets and at the little garden Hanneke had made.

Finally, the aunts got a chance to talk. They described
the bombing. Aunt Jo had waited it out under the stairs
with Hanneke, and Aunt Corrie had been in the city
with friends. They had heard the bombs whistling
before they struck. Aunt Jo insisted that she had seen
the wall move when a house had been hit only two
blocks away. All the windows had shattered, and Hanneke had shrieked in fear. She had been very upset, and
last night she had woke up screaming. She had gone
back to sleep only after Aunt Jo had taken her into bed
with her.

Aunt Corrie described the awful destruction that had
devastated the city. The entire city-center had been
leveled by bombs. Fire had done the rest, and its fury
still wasn't played out. People had fled in panic, aban-
doning their homes to the fire. Their only thought was
to escape with their lives. Firemen and soldiers had gone
out to fight the fire, but they were powerless in the face
of the raging flames.

Aunt Corrie told of all the refugees that had fled
by, afraid of further bombings. She told stories that
she had heard. An old woman's house had been hit,
and her apartment had come crashing down two whole
stories, but she had walked out of it unharmed. A
mother had found her child's hair sticking out of the
rubble of her home, and she had been able to free the
child, who was walking beside her unhurt. A family had
been trapped all night long in the cellar of a burning
house and hadn't been rescued until morning.

Suddenly they all jumped up in fright as a loud wail
came from the garden. The door burst open, and Han-

neke came running in, trembling from head to foot. She dove into Father's lap.

"An airplane, an airplane!" she screamed.

"Silly girl," said Father, laughing with relief. "It won't hurt you anymore. That's just the sound of its engines. The war's over!"

But Hanneke wouldn't listen, and it was some time before she calmed down.

Father quickly gulped down his coffee, however, and John could see that he was worried.

"We're going right back to Mommy," he said to Hanneke. "What do you think of that?" That seemed to help. She slid off Father's knee and rubbed at her eyes. "But you've got to be a big girl, because when we're in the car, we might see some more airplanes. But they won't hurt you. If you promise not to cry, we'll leave right away."

She promised eagerly, but her lips trembled.

Aunt Jo quickly packed her suitcase, and together they walked out to the car.

"Have you got enough gas?" asked Aunt Corrie. "The service stations have been ordered to close. It was on the news just this morning."

"Rats!" said Father. "That doesn't sound too good. We've got more than enough to get back to Scheveningen, but how are we going to get home tomorrow? Oh, well, maybe it will work out somehow. Hanneke, would you like to sit in the back seat with John?"

But little Hanneke was adamant about sitting on Father's lap. Because she was still distressed, Father thought it best to give in to her.

"John, you get behind the wheel," said Father. "Come on, Fritz. You get into the back seat."

"Do you think you should?" asked Aunt Jo anxiously.

"What? Let John drive, you mean? He's a safer driver than I am."

It was hard for John to look nonchalant. Under the amazed and anxious eyes of his aunts, he slid behind the wheel, started the car, waved, and put it in gear.

"Make sure you let us know how things turn out!" Aunt Corrie called after them. She was referring to Hanneke, of course.

They took the same road back, going in the same direction as the stream of refugees. An old woman put up her hand, so they took her along—her and her daughter, a caged canary, and a sackful of clothes. They had lost everything else, she said. They had grabbed a few things when a bomb fell on the building next door, and they had fled with what they could carry. The night had been spent outdoors in a park. Now they were on their way to Schiebroek, a small town just outside Rotterdam, where they hoped to find shelter with friends. But her picture of her dead husband, the picture hanging right next to the door, the only picture she had of him, had been left behind. And for this she wept.

When John dropped her off, she said to him, "Thank you very kindly, sir. What do I owe you?" And she tried to push a quarter into John's hand. John had a hard time leaving without having the tip forced on him.

The column of German trucks was still there

alongside the road. This time Fritz kept his tongue to himself. Most of the men lay sleeping in the grass now, and John drove by without slowing down. He kept thinking of Mother standing by the window or out on the steps, and he didn't notice the speedometer needle gradually climbing higher and higher until Father tapped on it.

They were approaching the first downed airplane. Father tried to divert Hanneke's attention, so that she wouldn't notice it. She had a little purse with a few pennies in it, and Father had her counting it over and over. But those big blue eyes didn't miss much. Fortunately, she didn't realize what the big structure was.

"What's that?" she asked. "A bridge?"

They didn't feel it necessary to correct her.

"And what's that over there?" she piped up again. "A cow?"

"It's a sackful of sand," said Father. The body of the animal was so swollen that it *did* look like a sackful of sand.

"It's not either," said Hanneke. "It had legs, and sacks don't have legs."

When everybody laughed at that, Hanneke joined in. They were making good time. They buzzed through Ypenburg, but then suddenly they were stopped. On the road stood a German soldier and a Dutch officer.

"I'm sorry, sir" said the officer. "You'll all have to get out except the driver. The car and the driver have to go back to Rotterdam to pick up the wounded."

"We'll go back right away," promised Father. "But first can't we bring this child to her mother? She just came from Rotterdam too."

"All right. Go ahead," said the officer and he saluted. The German raised his arm and barked, "Heil Hitler!" It was the first time they had heard the Nazi salute in person.

A few hundred meters down the road was another roadblock. This time it was manned by a noncom and a policeman. Again they were stopped and given the same order.

"We got permission from the officer up the road to bring this child home first," Father told him. "Then we'll come right back."

"You sure you'll come back?" the policeman asked skeptically.

"I promise," said Father, and they drove on. As they approached the bridge on the outskirts of The Hague, they were stopped for the third time. This time by a corporal.

"This car is needed in Rotterdam to pick up wounded," he said. "Turn it around!"

"We've got permission to bring this child home to her mother first," said Father. "It's not far. We'll be right back."

"I'm sorry, sir," said the soldier. "At least she's still got a mother. My wife and kids are still back there somewhere in that hell. Turn the car around! Right now! There's a bus stop on the other side of the bridge. Your kids can take the bus home."

"He's right," said Father. "Out boys. You're responsible for Hanneke. See that she gets home. I'm taking the car back."

But when Hanneke saw that Father was going to leave her with the two boys, she was seized by a fit of terror. No matter what Father said, she screamed and wept and clung to him so fiercely that he couldn't get behind the wheel. To make things worse, just then a couple of airplanes roared by overhead.

Father made a quick decision.

"Hush now," he said to Hanneke. "It's okay. Daddy's not leaving." He turned to John. "John, you get back in. Take it back to Rotterdam and lend all the help you can. I'm sure you'll run into someone who'll tell you what to do. You're on your own; I know you can handle it. Be careful and don't take any chances. Agreed?"

A shiver of fear went through John, but at the same time it was also a shiver of pride. For a moment he was dazed. Then suddenly he felt very calm. He was being called on to do something worthwhile, and he knew he could do it.

He looked at his father and said, "Don't worry, Dad. I can handle it." And he slid behind the wheel. Father handed him ten guilders through the open window.

"Here. You'll probably need some money. Get some gas if you've got the chance. You've got a good reason now—you're picking up the wounded."

Father quickly shook John's hand. Waving to Fritz and Hanneke, John turned the DKW back to Rotterdam. The soldier pointed him down another road that would take him through Delft.

Here he was, John De Boer, not even sixteen yet, and he was driving all by himself with an important mission in the ravaged city of Rotterdam.

CHAPTER NINE

Nevertheless, it was a scary feeling to be all alone in the car, driving off into the big world along strange roads, heading for a huge city that was almost completely unknown to him, a city, moreover, that was in flames. But he was soon over his moment of panic. After all, what an adventure! He might run into problems, but cross your bridges when you come to them, Father always said. As long as they came one at a time, he'd be able to handle them. He felt like singing, but before him hung the black curtain of smoke, and his mission was very serious: pick up the injured.

What if someone noticed that he was so young and asked him for his driver's license? But nobody seemed to be paying attention to such things. Policemen had more important things to do right now than to check driver's licenses. Maybe if he put on Father's sunglasses, he would look a couple of years older.

As he drove, he fished them out of the glove compartment and laid them down on the seat beside him, just in case. He didn't like wearing them; he'd rather see the world the way it really was. Without them he could keep a better eye out to see what there was to see. Here, too, there were parachutes and dead cows, and close to Delft a huge burnt-out factory lay smoldering.

He kept his speed down to 60 or 70 K.P.H. Driving conditions were excellent. There was very little traffic, and the route was well-marked through the city of Delft. Wait a minute—a service station on the right-hand side of the road! Quickly he braked and wheeled up to the pumps. He gave a short toot on the horn and a man in dirty overalls came ambling outside with his hands in his pockets; he slowly approached the car and stopped.

"Sorry, sir," (again someone had called him sir), "I can't help you. We're not supposed to pump any more gas. We were notified this morning!"

John called on the deepest voice he could muster. "I know," he said. "But I've got orders to pick up injured people in Rotterdam. How am I going to do that without gas?"

"Are you empty?"

"As good as," John exaggerated.

"Oh well," said the man. "What do I care?"And he lifted the hose off the hook.

"Check the oil?"

"That's okay. I'll take care of it."

John opened the hood and checked the oil. He kept a close eye on the numbers on the gas pump. "Careful!" he warned the attendant and the next moment gasoline gushed over the gas tank. At least it was full.

"You weren't anywhere near empty," the man said accusingly. "Oh well, why should I care?"

He dried off the car with a rag and screwed the gas cap back on.

"How much?" asked John taking out his wallet. The man didn't have change for a ten, so he went inside. When he came back he took a closer look at John and asked him, "How old are you?"

"Coming on nineteen," John said with a straight face. "At least, I hope so."

"You sure look young for your age," said the man. "But why should I care? Why should I care about anything? The Krauts are going to get it all anyway. I wish my boy was home. He was stationed on the Grebbe Line, and we haven't heard a thing."

John nodded sympathetically.

"I hope you hear something soon," he said as he started the car. "And thanks for the gas."

The man didn't respond but only stared somberly off into the distance as John drove away. John got back on the road and increased his speed a little. The gas tank was full; they should be able to make it to Drenthe with gas to spare. Father would be proud of him.

He would soon be in the city. The sun disappeared behind the smoke, glowing red through the haze. It cast an ominous hue over the landscape. But now he had to stop looking at the sky and begin to pay close attention to where he was going. The roads were getting busier. John had no idea where he was headed, but he drove on, hoping for someone to give him directions.

"I'm sure you'll run into someone who will tell you what to do," Father had said. But who? There were plenty of people about—many had their mouths and noses covered with handkerchiefs against the smoke—but everyone hurried on. So John went on too. The smoke was getting worse, and the air was filled with small bits of ash that came floating down on the car. John turned up his window and drove on slowly.

Suddenly he came upon the first signs of the bombing. In the middle of a street full of apartments gaped a big empty space. One wall of the building was still standing so that the adjoining building had not been damaged. But on the other side, the roof of the adjacent building had been pulled down into the chasm. The street was filled with rubble. Had people been killed in that building? No one could have lived through such an explosion!

Careful! An old man with an armload of blankets crossed the street right in front of the car. Sometimes visibility was dangerously low. The people looked like shadows in the smoke. Down the road, on the other side of the intersection, flames were shooting out of an apartment building. Firemen and policemen moved about in the murky street, but there were no onlookers. A young fellow wearing a white armband was just crossing the street. John drove up to him and stuck his head out the window.

"Hey, pardon me! I was sent from The Hague to pick up injured people," he said. "Can you tell me where I'm supposed to go?"

"Yeah, sure," he said. "There's a hospital ship on the

Meuse River. That would be your best bet." And he began giving John directions how to get there, but they were so involved that John couldn't make much sense of them.

"You know what?" said the fellow. "I'll ride along with you and point out the way. You must be a stranger here."

He got in beside John. The ship wasn't far away, but it was hard to get to. In some places, huge piles of rubble blocked the way, so John had to detour from street to street. In one street, a house was burning like a torch, showering sparks over the whole block.

"You can get by," said the young fellow. But John could still smell the spilt gas in the car, and he preferred to make another detour rather than take any risks.

"They can't stop the fire." said John's passenger. "It's an impossible job. If only the wind would die down or we would get a good rain. When one of those burning buildings collapses, a mass of sparks goes shooting up like a volcano, and they scatter over the whole neighborhood. Most of the people have fled, and the windows have been knocked out by the bombings.

"Like over there. Look! The curtains are fluttering out through the broken window. One spark in that lace and—whoosh!—another place goes up in flames. You should see how quickly that goes. It's unbelievable! Right—turn right here. You can't get by up ahead. There's too much rubble."

By the Meuse the smoke wasn't quite as dense. The sun sparkled cheerfully on the water, but on both banks smoldered the ruins of buildings. On the far bank, downriver a few hundred yards, lay the burnt-out hulk of a large ship.

"That's the *Statendam*," said John's guide. "The hospital ship is over there. Now you don't need me anymore. Let me off here and then I can hitch a ride back with that truck."

John drove the car as close as possible to the ship, which lay tied up to the wharf. It had huge red crosses on its sides and also on the deck. John went up the gangplank and knocked on a door.

Inside, a doctor in a white coat was busy bandaging a young girl with a deep scalp wound. She sat on a stool, leaning forward over a white table. Her dress was smeared with blood. She moaned softly. A nurse was unwrapping another bandage. The doctor talked as he worked, his hands in constant motion.

"Wounded for The Hague? Go to Eudokia. We've sent many people over there. Do you know where Eudokia Hospital is? Don't you know your way around here at all? We'll have to send someone along. Is Rita still around?"

The nurse left and returned a few minutes later with a young student nurse. The latter had a friendly, open look and met John with a smile.

"If you wait a minute, you can take this girl home at the same time," the doctor told John. "She lives out that way."

John didn't have to wait long. The young nurse was soon leading the bandaged girl to the parked DKW. The girl was a bit wobbly on her feet, but she managed a weak smile.

"Won't my mother be surprised!" she said, as if it were a joke. "I went back to our place to see if I could find our cat. We left her behind when we fled yesterday. But the house was gone. It took me a long time to find the place where it was yesterday. The ashes were still warm, but I climbed over them to see if I could find our cat. Suddenly, down I went into the cellar. Junk came tumbling in after me and then—whammo!—something hit me on the head. What happened after that, I have no idea. Do you know who found me and brought me to the doctor?"

The pretty nurse had no idea either.

"Did you people lose everything?"

"Everything. But the important thing is, our whole family got out safely. We were standing together in the hall when the bombs started falling. Now we're staying in the home of a family that took refuge in a bomb shelter. They were all killed by a direct hit, but their house wasn't even touched!"

"Stop!" cried the nurse, but John was already slamming on the brakes. Directly in front of them, a house was burning, and people were running in all directions. One man almost ran into the car. The front wall of the house was teetering; then it began to lean forward—slowly at first, and then faster and faster, until it buckled and came crashing down into the street. A cloud of dust, smoke and sparks went surging up. John rammed the car into reverse and went speeding backwards, but the cloud overtook them and enveloped the car in partial darkness.

"That was close!" said the nurse. "You might as well

turn around; you'll never get by that. Turn right at the corner. I know another way to get there!"

Soon the nurse was helping the bandaged girl out of the car in front of her temporary home. She returned almost immediately.

"Now to Eudokia," she said.

On they went again. Down some streets that had no damage at all and then between ruins that emitted a choking haze which penetrated into the car even with the windows closed. In the middle of one block, a woman wearing an apron stepped out into the street and waved down the car. John stopped. Did she need a ride?

"Did you people see my husband?" the woman quavered. "I haven't seen him since yesterday. Nobody has seen him! He's wearing blue overalls. He was going to help fight the fires, he said. He was supposed to be back before dark, but I spent the whole night alone with the kids."

"Don't worry ma'am. He'll turn up," said the nurse. "But we'll keep an eye out for him. That's a promise!"

She signaled John to drive on, but the woman clung to the open window.

"His name's Verbeek," she cried. "Hank Verbeek. He's thirty-six years old, and he's got a mole on his left cheek right by his ear. Please find him and tell him to come home. What am I going to do without him in this hell?"

"Go!" urged the nurse. And as they pulled away, she explained, "Hundreds of people are out searching like that. But there's nothing to be done, at least not right now. Maybe he'll turn up at home all of a sudden, and maybe he's lying somewhere under a collapsed wall. Then he'll be found later."

Now her face looked pale and drawn. By the time they got to Eudokia, however, she was smiling again. She was in and out of the hospital in short order and slid back into the car next to him.

"No luck," she said. "They don't need us here. All the wounded that they couldn't put up here have been taken away. But I'll take you to a big chemical plant. It's quite a distance from here. They said it was still supposed to be filled with injured people."

Again they picked their way through the city, between high hills of rubble and twisted iron, past fragments of walls and broken furniture. Driving took all of John's concentration, for in some places he could hardly squeeze by the debris that cluttered the streets. He was working up quite a sweat, and he kept wiping his face with his handkerchief.

He was relieved when they came to a divided boulevard that hadn't been hit at all. In the broad park between the streets, whole families had set up house. Some had made roofs of canvas and blankets. One woman was cooking at a camp stove. Elsewhere, smoke rose from a small fire. Children played together on the grass. And a man was chopping wood.

A few kilometers down the road, they came upon another column of German military vehicles parked on the shoulder: armored cars, all kinds of artillery, trucks of the motorized infantry, and supply trucks. The soldiers were crowding around a couple of carts that were selling lemonade, beer, and hot chocolate. One of the peddlers had painted the words "Ice Cold Beer" on his cart in German. He was doing a booming business.

"Look at him," said the young nurse in disgust. "As soon as there's money to be made, enemies suddenly turn into friends. Those peddlers already seem to have forgotten what the Germans did to Rotterdam. But I'll never forget!"

Her face suddenly looked very intense, but only for a few moments. She couldn't stay angry or sad for very long.

"My stomach is growling," she said. "No wonder! It's almost 1:30 and I haven't had a bite to eat since 4 o'clock this morning."

"What?" said John in surprise. "Since 4 o'clock? Have you been on duty since then?"

"On duty!" she laughed. "Not on duty, but I've been kept busy all night long. But I'm doing all right. Look over there! I think they've set up a feeding station over there. Let's go take a look. I'll bet you're hungry too!"

"You bet!" said John eagerly. "My stomach's not just growling, it's barking!"

A large crowd of people was gathered around the building where food was being distributed. But her nursing uniform gave Rita the right to elbow her way to the door ahead of the others. Soon she emerged with a couple of buns, a piece of sausage, and a chunk of cheese. She gave John a triumphant smile.

"She sure has an attractive and friendly face," thought John. Maybe he ought to mention those smudges on her forehead, but they really only made her look prettier.

"We'd better get going," she said. "I'll feed you while you're driving."

"As they traveled on, Rita shoved pieces of bread, cheese, and sausage into his mouth. Before they had finished eating, they arrived at their destination—a huge factory. John stopped, and Rita quickly dumped the leftovers into his lap.

"Here, you finish this. I've had enough to keep me going for a while."

She disappeared into the building. After John had waited a long time and she still hadn't come back, he went in through the door that she had entered. He stepped into a long, broad hallway. One of the doors opened into a huge area. It contained an incredible chaos of army cots and oddments of furniture, between and on and under which hundreds of people lay and sat and walked. Many families had found temporary refuge here.

"Isn't this cozy?" the voice of the young nurse, Rita, said at his shoulder. "But all the injured have been moved from here too. They're all gone. And they don't know where else to send us."

"Couldn't they phone?" asked John.

Rita gave him a you've-got-to-be-kidding kind of look. "They'd love to phone, but sad to say, telephone lines aren't immune to bombs. There's no gas and water either. But I don't think phoning around would do much good anyway. They said that all kinds of cars had been sent here for nothing."

"Well, I guess we're too late," said John slowly. "They must have been just ordering cars to come out here willy-nilly!"

"It looks that way," said Rita. "But, better too many than not enough. I guess you'd better bring me back to the ship, and then you can go back home."

"I hope they don't send me back again when I get to The Hague," John remarked, grinning ruefully.

"I'll get one of the doctors to give you a note saying that we don't need any more cars," Rita decided.

Soon they were back in the city again, but this time they detoured around the city center so that they could drive on virtually unhindered.

The doctor on the ship scribbled an almost illegible note for John, and Rita walked him back to the car to thank him.

"You're a terrific driver!" she said. "And I'll bet you're not much older than seventeen."

John didn't contradict her, but he felt a blush beginning to climb up from his collar.

"I'm not much older either." She laughed. "I only just turned eighteen. Do you live in The Hague?"

"No, in Drenthe," he said, admiring her smile. He told her the name of the village close to their new home.

"Oh, I've been there," she said. "I've got an aunt who lived in Groningen, and we've cycled through there. I wouldn't mind riding up there with you in this cute little car. You think you could put up with my company?" She asked this with a mischievous grin and her eyes sparkled with humor.

"Hey, that would be neat!" said John. "I'd like that. But drop by if you're ever up there. I'm sure everybody would love to meet you."

She promised she would, shook his hand, and darted off to the ship. She turned around once more and shouted at him, "Go straight ahead until you get to the railroad crossing and then turn left. You'll be out of the city in no time. Bye!"

He waited until she had disappeared inside, and then he waited a few more minutes to see if she would reappear. But she was gone.

So he started the car and drove off. He was singing; he felt on top of the world. "Rita," he said to himself. She was nice! He hoped that she would drop in on them in Drenthe sometime soon. He should have asked her for her address; then he could have written her. He was sure that she would write back. He'd like to get to know her better. She thought he was seventeen! What if she knew that he wasn't even sixteen yet? Then she wouldn't want to be his girl for sure.

Oh oh, had he already passed the railroad crossing? He hadn't been watching where he was driving. He had better get hold of himself. What if his folks knew that he was already daydreaming about a girl—and one that was two years older than himself!

"Don't be silly," Father would say. "There's plenty of time for that later." And he'd be right. But she was sure nice, and pretty too!

Suddenly he found himself in the middle of rubble again. Once he had to back up because he couldn't get through. He asked for directions from a man who was pushing a large cart loaded high with household goods.

The man wanted to direct him back through the city, but he didn't feel like going there again.

He began driving up one street and down another, until suddenly he recognized the neighborhood. He was on the road to Hillegersberg, where his two aunts lived. Ahead was the tunnel. So his aunts' place was only a few blocks away. Should he stop by for a minute? Wouldn't they be surprised if they found him standing at the front door!

He hesitated for a moment. His folks would be looking for him pretty soon; he really shouldn't waste any more time. It must be close to 3 o'clock. He took the narrow country road that Father had taken. People were still hauling all kinds of boxes and baggage along the road. But this time they were heading in both directions. Some people seemed to be returning to the city. Nobody stopped him. At this rate, he should be home in about half an hour.

But his estimate proved wrong. When he got onto the main highway, he found himself in the middle of the German army. A convoy of all kinds of military vehicles stretched out as far as the eye could see in both directions; trucks full of laughing soldiers, supply trucks, artillery, armored cars, tanks—a rumbling, clanging, rattling, sputtering, thundering occupation parade.

They moved slowly along the road to The Hague. Messengers went roaring by on huge motorcycles, telling some vehicles to speed up and holding up others. They delivered their orders and went swerving in and out at breakneck speed between the army vehicles.

John drove along somewhere in the middle of the convoy, almost deafened by the clamor. Nobody paid the slightest attention to him. Sometimes he managed to

pass a whole row of trucks, keeping an anxious eye out for an opening to dart back into if a motorcycle came tearing from the opposite direction.

The convoy had to wait about half an hour at the spot where the airplane lay across the road. That obstacle had to be moved to make room for the tanks to get by. At Delft they were held up even longer, as a long convoy came out of the city to join theirs.

Later, he saw an opportunity to pass several tanks. Those rambling monsters emitted such an overwhelming din that it reverberated through everything. The steering wheel vibrated in his hands. The lead tank suddenly swerved to avoid something on the road and John found himself on the shoulder. That frightened him, and he decided to stay in line the rest of the way.

Thus, he entered The Hague as part of the victorious German army. Here and there, small groups of people stood cheering and waving at the German soldiers. It startled John for a moment. But then he thought, "Oh, of course. Dutch Nazis!"

John slipped away into a side street and pulled over, exhausted. He had to get out for a minute because the houses were beginning to spin before his eyes. He strolled back to the intersection, wiping the sweat from his face with his sleeve. Apparently he had lost his handkerchief somewhere. He saw a German soldier snapping pictures of a group of enthusiastic Dutchmen.

"Those miserable traitors!" he heard a man say who was also looking on. "I'll bet that gets into the German papers: 'Our Soldiers Welcomed in Liberated Holland.' It's enough to make you vomit!"

A woman standing next to him elbowed him. "Ssht!" she warned, eyeing John suspiciously. But John smiled at her and nodded. Then she smiled back.

He noticed that some people were grinning at each other and looking at him. Was there something wrong with him? He checked his clothes, but he couldn't find anything out of the ordinary. He got back in the car and looked for a way to get home that bypassed the city center. It was about 6 o'clock when he drove up to the house and set the DKW in its old parking spot.

Everybody came running outside to welcome him: Father, Mother, Fritz, Uncle Herman, and Tricia. They were laughing and happy as they grabbed him and began plying him with questions.

"Boy, you're dirty!" one of them exclaimed.

"You smell like smoke!" said another.

"Look at that!" said Father. "You can see where he's been." He pointed to a large black spot on the linen top of the DKW. He had been on fire without realizing it!

Hanneke also came out on the steps.

"Mom, Daddy!" she cried fearfully and looked around, half panicked. When she saw them, she made a dash for her mother and insisted on being held like a baby.

"How's she doing!" John asked anxiously.

Mother nodded. "She'll be all right," she whispered. "She's still a little upset, but that's understandable. She's gone through a lot."

"You go and clean up now, John," said Aunt Haddie. "Supper's ready. We can all sit down and eat."

When John went into the bedroom and looked in the

mirror, he understood why the people in town had laughed. He was as black as a chimney sweep. His face was smeared with a layer of soot mingled with sweat. His neck, too, was etched with thick black lines. It felt wonderful to splash cool water over his face and neck. He felt like a new man.

Supper had never tasted so good. And he had to tell everything that he had seen. He said hardly anything about Rita, the young nurse, but it was enough to set Tricia giggling and teasing and nudging the others. He pinned her down on the sofa, but she squirmed out of his grasp and ran into the kitchen. He stayed on the sofa, stretched out full length; he hadn't realized how tired he really was.

Later, he heard Jacobs come in and say that according to the radio the number of dead in Rotterdam wasn't nearly as high as had been feared—only a few hundred. But Aunt Corrie had said thousands. Moreover, the Germans had broken their word. They had set an ultimatum period for surrender, but they hadn't even waited for that time to expire before they began their vicious attack on the city.

But John had stopped listening. He was driving down one of the beautiful country roads in Drenthe, and he was smiling at the pretty young nurse sitting beside him.

CHAPTER TEN

They had planned to get an early start the next morning, but there was much packing and checking to be done, and they had a hard time arranging everything to fit inside the car. So it was 9 o'clock before the car stood in front of the door, ready to go. Then they still had to go to several of the neighbors to say goodbye, and Father suddenly remembered that John still had to pay back the twenty-five guilders to the man with the fat wife. They could get along without it now that they were going home.

John ran to the shopping area and came panting into the little store. The chubby owner stood behind the counter helping a couple of customers and talking about the war.

"I don't doubt it for a minute. One day we'll see the Queen and the House of Orange back in The Hague. 'Oso,' I say when I meet a loyal countryman, 'Orange

Shall Overcome! Oso!' Even though I'm no Edison, that's my invention. Hey, here's my friend with the good news from Zeist. How are you? What can I do for you?"

"We're going home!" said John. "And I came to return your money. My father says thanks and the best to you and your wife. And he said if you ever need anything . . . ."

But the man wouldn't take the money. "You might need it on the way back," he insisted. So John dropped it on the counter along with one of Father's business cards.

The friendly shopkeeper accompanied him to the door with his hand on John's shoulder. He said something about fellow countrymen helping each other, and as John hurried down the street, he shouted after him, "Oso!" and stuck up his thumb.

"Oso?" John wondered, befuddled. And then he remembered the conversation in the store: "Orange Shall Overcome—Oso!"

"Neat!" thought John. No one who didn't already know would catch on to what it meant. As soon as he got back, he tried it on Uncle Herman and Tricia. When Mr. Schram came outside and jumped on his bike, John couldn't resist giving him the thumbs-up sign and shouting, "Oso! Mr. Schram!"

But maybe because he was dressed in his police uniform or because he was used to being shunned, the man didn't answer. He only gave John a nasty look. He also fixed an evil eye on the loaded DKW and on Father, who was talking to some neighbors. John felt a sudden surge of dislike for the man.

Hah! What did he care about that skinny old rabbit-face! He would probably never see him again. They were going home; the war was over! His new room and his books, the new house and the garden and the orchàrd awaited him. It would be nice and peaceful out in the country.

They were calling him! The others were already getting into the car. He said a quick goodbye and squeezed into the back seat. Half the neighborhood gathered around to wave goodbye. They had made quite a few friends in the short time of their stay with Uncle Herman and Aunt Haddie. Mother consoled little Jobie Jacobs with the promise that he could come and stay with them during the summer vacation and visit Fritz. Uncle Herman and Aunt Haddie would bring him when they came to visit.

Then they were moving.

"Oso!" yelled John, giving the thumbs-up sign out of the back window, and everyone waved until they turned the corner.

The car was actually much too small for a family of seven. Mother sat in the front beside Father and had Hanneke on her lap. John, Tricia, and Fritz sat shoulder to shoulder in the back, and Trudy hopped from one lap to the next until she finally discovered that she could sit and play with her doll on the floor between their feet. Usually the cramped quarters caused quite a few spats between the children, but this time everyone seemed resigned to an uncomfortable day. Even Fritz was quiet and snuggled into his own corner as tightly as possible.

Father took the highway to Utrecht. He figured that

the old ferry at Hattem would probably be back in service. It was the shortest way home. The little DKW purred contentedly down the four-lane highway to Gouda and from there to Woerden. Soon they came to the place where the whole countryside was flooded on both sides of the road. They drove between gleaming expanses of water for several kilometers.

"These are the water defenses," said Father. "They could just as well have saved themselves the trouble."

But it had been done. It would be weeks or even months before the land could be reclaimed. For the farmers in this area, it was a catastrophe.

Not far from Utrecht they passed a group of Dutch soldiers, prisoners of war, who were being herded along by armed German soldiers. They shuffled along wearily under the hot sun; they had probably come a long way already.

After passing them, Father pulled over to the side of the road. "Give me all the chocolate bars that you've got, Mother," he said. "And see what else we've got to eat. There are also a few packages of cigarettes in that bag. We've got to show these boys that we're still with them!"

They got out of the car and waited for the approaching soldiers. Would the Germans object if they handed the Dutch soldiers something? No, they looked on benignly as Father and Mother handed out the snacks to the troop of prisoners, who perked up noticeably.

"Never fear," shouted one of the men. "We'll be back!"

"Oso!" answered John, holding up his thumb. "Orange Shall Overcome—Oso!" By their grins he could tell that they had caught on. When they passed the group for the second time a couple of minutes later, several of the men gave them the thumbs-up sign.

In Utrecht they had to wait for a long column of German vehicles. Here too the German army was advancing into the heart of Holland. Except for John, this was the first time that they had seen the German juggernaut on the move. The military might of the enemy made a great impression on the whole family. Sobbing, Hanneke crawled up against Mother and tried to hide from the deafening clanging.

They drove into Zeist, their old home town. Father wanted to fill up with gas at their old service station. The attendant told them that they would need a travel permit from the mayor in order to go on. While Father went to the town hall, John drove the rest of the family to where they had lived until ten days ago. They planned to visit with their old neighbors until Father returned.

Ten days ago? It seemed much longer. So much had happened in those few days! There were endless stories to be heard about the grisly dramas that had been played out along the Grebbe Line. The hospitals in town were crowded with wounded soldiers.

As soon as they had stopped, Fritz disappeared with some friends and showed up a little later only to ask if he could stay for dinner with one of them. The rest of the family had also been invited to stay and eat. In the meantime, Father arrived with the travel permit, and he let himself be persuaded to accept the invitation.

It was almost 2 o'clock before they got back on the road. But they didn't have to stop anywhere else, so they should be home in a few hours—at least if the ferry at Katerveer was in operation. Nobody in Zeist seemed to know.

They passed through Amersfoort. The city looked like a ghost town. All the people had been evacuated because it had been an important military objective in the war. In one of the town squares that they drove through, a huge pile of half-burnt uniforms and other army supplies still emitted acrid smoke. The town of Nykerk, ten kilometers down the highway, had been hard hit by the war, and much of it had been destroyed. But on the other side of Nykerk there was little evidence of warfare.

The hot afternoon sun made them all tired and impatient to reach the ferry. Then they could all get out of the car and stretch their cramped arms and legs. As they approached the Yssel River at Hattem, they could see the beautiful arches of the bridge lying broken in the water. But there was no sign of a ferry, just a small boat plying back and forth with room for two bicycles at most.

"Try Kampen," said a local man. "There's supposed to be a ferry operating there."

So they crawled back into the DKW and detoured to Kampen. As they drew near the city, they could see a ferry crossing the river. But a long row of German trucks stood waiting their turn to cross. Father drove to the end of the line, but he was waved away.

"Come back early tomorrow morning," said a German officer.

Tomorrow? Father had no intention of waiting until tomorrow. What were they supposed to do in the meantime? Rent rooms in Kampen?

"Try the drawbridge in Deventer," suggested a policeman. "The Germans have it working again."

"Are you sure?" asked Father.

"I spoke to somebody who crossed it this morning," said the policeman. "He was a dentist, so he ought to know about bridges," the officer added with a grin.

But Father didn't respond. The thought of making such a long detour was very discouraging. But everyone was eager to go. After stopping at a cafe for lemonade, they resumed their journey with new vigor.

The cold lemonade, however, seemed to have done Tricia no good, for she suddenly complained that she didn't feel well. It was a good thing that Father stopped right away, because Tricia lurched out of the car and vomited into the ditch.

She returned a minute later, looking pale but smiling, and as cheerfully as she could she said, "Let's go! Now we should be able to make better time. I lost a few pounds back there." She was quite a girl!

The drawbridge was in operation. A big fat German officer blocked the road, however. It scared them for a moment, and John suddenly thought of the revolver. Did Father have it in his pocket? But the soldier only held out his hand and said, "Fifty cents for toll."

Mother was outraged. "Making us pay to cross our own bridge! And in our own country!"

But Father laughed. "Easy, honey," he said. "If a few quarters makes you mad, you're in for a bad time. I'm sure we'll be paying a lot more to the Germans before this is all over!"

Cutting across the middle of Overysel, Father aimed at Ommen; but he was worried about the bridge at Vecht. If it had been blown up, they would have to make another long detour. Before they reached Vecht, however, they were stopped by a small creek. The bridge had been completely destroyed. The opposite bank was only a few meters away, but it might as well have been a few kilometers. But two boys who happened to be passing by told them that if they followed the river a short way they would find another bridge, still intact.

So they followed the boys' directions. They ended up on a soft dirt road with deep ruts. Although Father drove carefully,one minute he would be dropping into potholes, and the next lurching over clumps of grass. John noticed that Father kept looking at Mother, and a couple of times he asked her, "You all right, honey? You sure it's not too rough?"

"Why don't we stop here and stretch our legs a little, Father?" asked John. "It's so beautiful. Tricia could use some fresh air. She's starting to look a little sickish again."

"John's right," said Tricia with an apologetic laugh. "I'm not feeling very well."

"Not a bad idea," agreed Father and immediately stopped the car.

"You all get out and walk," he said, "and I'll drive on to the bridge and wait for you there."

But as Father started to drive off, the wheels sank away into the loose sand and spun uselessly. The car was stuck. John and Fritz got behind it and pushed. Finally, it rocked free and went shooting ahead. Father drove away.

It was a beautiful walk. Trudy and Fritz picked flowers along the creek, and John offered Mother his arm to help her navigate the bumpy road. When they caught up to Father, all of them had revived considerably and had worked the knots out of their legs.

The rest of the trip went smoothly. The bridge in Ommen was not damaged, so there were no further delays. They began to ask themselves anxiously, "What will the house look like when we get there? Has there been any fighting in the neighborhood? What if the house has been damaged? What will we do if our new house is destroyed?"

Everyone was quiet, wrapped in his own thoughts. When the car was finally headed down the country road toward their new home, it was late evening. The red sun was balanced on the horizon, spreading its color over the countryside.

The evening light cast its soft hues on the white walls of their new home; it stood peacefully among the trees, undamaged.

Beside the house, on a chair tilted back against the wall, sat Uncle Gerrit smoking his pipe. Nemo, their dog, lay sleeping at his feet. They made an idyllic country scene. Margy came hurrying out through the kitchen door, still carrying her knitting.

"Coffee's ready!" called Uncle Gerrit, as if they had just returned from a short drive in the country.

CHAPTER ELEVEN

They had been home for more than two months. To John it seemed as though nothing had happened. Life went on as before. The local farmers did their work as usual. Uncle Gerrit, too, was busy every day: he sprayed the fruit trees and cared for the flower and vegetable gardens. He was always in a good mood and ready to crack a joke. Trudy followed him around or sat with Mother in the summerhouse. When Mother sewed, Trudy sat beside her with a needle and thread and stabbed at a scrap of cloth as if it were her livelihood.

Hanneke was attending school and was as cheerful as ever. Occasionally at night when an airplane droned by overhead, she would awake in a fright and would wail for Mother. This fear would probably stay with her for some time, the doctor had said, but otherwise there was nothing to worry about.

The other three children pedaled their bikes to school

every day: Fritz to grade school, Tricia and John to high school. Father was busy drawing plans for a large country home to be built in the area. But whenever he traveled, he went by bus or train, for the car had been put up on blocks. A special permit was required to use a car, and Father hadn't even tried to qualify. This was okay with John, for often those who had permits were suspected of being Nazi sympathizers, unless it was absolutely essential to their work.

After the tension and fear of the war, the peacefulness of the country was a blessing to all of them.

"Life here is so beautiful," thought John. Every day was a delight. His new room was just the way he liked it. He was also happy with his new school, and he had already found a couple of friends who made good companions. He was again taking judo lessons. And on his sixteenth birthday, Mother and Father had given him a fine camera.

"Soon they won't be available anymore," Father had said. "The Germans will confiscate them all."

During this time John would have preferred to forget that they were still at war. After all, nothing had changed; everything went on as usual. True, an Austrian turncoat named Seyss-Inquart ("Inky-Heart" Uncle Gerrit called him) had been appointed commissioner of the country and had delivered a speech from the same hall in The Hague where the Queen made her annual speech from the throne.

This had struck the people as outrageously arrogant and rude. But what he had *said* hadn't been so bad. The Germans had not come to oppress the Dutch, he said, and the liberty of the Netherlands would be restored. In the future they would be able to decide for themselves how they were to be governed, and so on. Besides, the German soldiers hadn't turned out to be so bad either. They were well-behaved on the streets and bothered no one. They paid for everything that they bought. In fact, it was said that a German soldier who had stolen a bicycle had been shot for his petty crime.

Moreover, all Dutch prisoners of war had been released. Even the ones who had been shipped to Germany had returned. The newspapers laid it on a bit thick, to be sure, talking about the magnanimity of the Fuehrer. But it could not be denied that the Germans were doing their utmost to make friends with the Dutch. Some said that they were buying everything in sight and cleaning out the stores. And farmers were ordered to deliver cattle and horses to the Germans. But everyone got paid, and they were paid better prices than before the war.

Meanwhile, the war continued. The Belgian and French armies had also been defeated by the Germans. The English had been saved only by a frantic retreat from Dunkirk. Hitler had made a peace proposal to England, but Churchill had emphatically rejected it. The free world would fight until Germany had been vanquished, he said. Now the Germans had begun their horrible bombings of London and other English cities. It would probably not be long before they crossed the North Sea and invaded England too.

"Forward! On to England!" sang the German soldiers as they marched down the city streets. And groups of boys tagged along singing, "Splish, splash! Splish, splash!" Most people were sure that if the Germans did try to invade England, they would end up on the bottom of the North Sea. It was a favorite topic of conversation, but John quickly tired of it. The newspapers were filled with news about the war, but you didn't have to read them if you didn't want to.

Nor did you have to listen to the radio, which only broadcasted what the Germans wanted you to hear. The radio stood in the living room but was seldom turned on. Except at night. Then Father listened to broadcasts from England over the BBC. But John had no desire to listen. Besides, he couldn't understand them anyway.

Later, a Dutch station also began to broadcast from England—Radio Orange. Then Fritz joined Father and Uncle Gerrit around the radio at night and chattered excitedly about what he heard. But John was too busy with other things. Life was too beautiful to let it be spoiled by war news.

"Let them fight their wars if they think it's such fun," he said to himself. "I'm staying out of it. They can do it without me. I'll study hard, learn to take good pictures, and enjoy nature. That miserable war can go hang! There's nothing that *I* can do about it anyway." Many others felt just like John.

One afternoon, one of John's friends, Carl van Bergen, who was one grade ahead of him, invited John home with him and took him upstairs where he had fixed up a small studio. Carl was an accomplished artist. He showed John a drawing on which he had been busy for several days.

"What do you think of it?" he asked.

It was a pen drawing of a house with a smashed door, shattered windows, and bullet holes in the walls. At the table—obviously in the mother's chair, for her darning was still on the table—sat the German soldier who had broken in. He was eating greedily. Clinging together in the background, stood several children, watching him with angry and frightened faces. The soldier devouring the family's food had the face of Seyss-Inquart.

One of the children, a little boy with weepy eyes and a fawning attitude, leaned against the German's knee and pointed accusingly at his brothers and sisters. Another snub-nosed, rosy-cheeked youngster—"He looks almost like Fritz," thought John—was sneaking up behind the soldier. He had his eye on the gun and holster that hung on the back of the chair. The caption over the cartoon read: "Our New Daddy!"

John laughed, marveling at Carl's skill.

"That's great, man!" he exclaimed. "How'd you ever dream it up? Especially that sniveling little Nazi in his black suit! He's the black sheep of the family, eh? But who is that little kid behind the German?"

"Can't you guess?" asked Carl, studying John's face closely. "Well, you'll probably catch on some day." And he started to put the cartoon away, as if that were the end of the matter.

"You know what?" said John suddenly. "You ought to draw more of these. I wouldn't mind having one myself. The more people that see your cartoons, the better. Lots of people are being taken in by the friendly act of the Germans. That's what my dad says. If we could

figure out a way to get a whole bunch of these printed . . . ."

Carl burst out laughing. He got up, walked to the far
end of the room and rolled up a corner of the carpet.
Then he pried up one of the floorboards, reached down
and lifted out a whole stack of drawings—all copies of
the one he had just showed John. They were quite a bit
smaller, but they were sharp and clear, better even than
John could have imagined.

"Here," said Carl, "take some. I knew I had you sized
up right. My friends weren't sure that you were awake
to what's happening. But I knew there was more to you
than that. That's why I took you home with me. Spread
those cartoons wherever you can. But be careful! Make
sure no one sees you. It's illegal, of course. If you're
caught, you might end up in jail. The Krauts already
know about it. Some numbskull was stupid enough to
drop one in the mailbox of the S.D., the German police.
I'm not sure that they appreciate my sense of humor."
Carl grinned.

With the cartoons hidden between the pages of his
atlas and safely tucked away in his knapsack, John
pedaled for home. He suddenly saw the world with different eyes. Something stirred inside him—something
that he had also felt during those days in Scheveningen.
He was doing something again! He was helping in the
struggle against the enemy.

At home he immediately showed the cartoons to
Father. Father thought that they were tremendous, and
he helped John to send them to people in every corner of
the country. They stuffed them into envelopes without a

return address. The next morning, John mailed them in town on his way to school.

Now it was two weeks later. John had received a letter from Rita, the young nurse. Her name wasn't on it, but it had been mailed in Rotterdam and was signed, "Your passenger of May 15th." The letter was full of satirical verse about Hitler, Seyss-Inquart, and other prominent Nazis. There were also several patriotic poems. Fritz and Tricia got the biggest kick out of a mocking little song about Hitler's ambition to invade England. The story was making the rounds that the Germans had mistaken a long pier being built into the English Channel for a bridge to England. A little later, Fritz was sitting in the back yard singing loudly:

> Help me, my Feuhrer!
> My blood can't be purer;
> My heart's made of starch—
> But please stop this march!
>
> My will's made of iron
> Like the rockets we're firin';
> But let's stop, if you please!
> It's up over my knees!
>
> We'll carry our war
> To Churchill's front door;
> But my future looks grim,
> 'Cause this German can't swim!

Help me, my Fuehrer!
As England gets nearer,
My heart's filled with fear
For the bridge isn't here!

Father had to warn Fritz not to sing so loud. A couple of passers-by stopped on the road to listen and laugh at the lyrics. But Father was afraid that some Nazi sympathizer might come by and hear Fritz.

John immediately sent Rita one of Carl's cartoons. He didn't know her address, so he wrote on the envelope: Hospital Ship, Rotterdam. "That should do it," he thought. And it did, for one week later he got a post card with Rita's address on it. She must have decided that it was safer to get such mail at home. At last John knew where she lived.

One day they suddenly had a boarder. He introduced himself as Van Vliet and was wearing an ordinary suit when he arrived. But it didn't take John long to figure out that the man was an army officer—Captain Van Dyk, the old school chum whom Father had met in The Hague. He had been on General Winkelman's staff. First, John couldn't figure out why the man had to use a phony name. He spent a great deal of time talking with Father in the studio. When he left, the two men had given each other an unusually long handshake and had looked deep into one another's eyes. "Just as if they were making a pledge," thought John.

Uncle Gerrit had mused, "He's quite a fellow, that Van Vliet. As long as we've got men like that, we're far from conquered!"

A few days later, Father invited John to join him for a dip in the canal.

"Why in the canal?" asked John. "I thought you said it wasn't healthy to go swimming in the canal, and that we ought to use the swimming pool."

"Come along, and you'll see," said Father.

"Isn't Fritz coming?" asked John as they were leaving.

"No," said Father. "The less he knows about it, the better."

It was all very secretive. They rode their bikes along the canal for a few kilometers until they got to a lonely stretch. And who should be sitting on the bank fishing but Uncle Gerrit! John was surprised to see him; he didn't seem to be the fisherman type.

"Ha!" he said. "You're just the people I wanted to see! Maybe you two will have better luck. I haven't even had a nibble. Maybe the fish have been scared off by something on the bottom."

"Is this the place?" asked Father.

"As near as I can figure out," said the old man. "I may be off ten meters or so, but not much more."

As they undressed, Father told John what they were looking for. Here, on the bottom of the canal, there were supposed to be quite a number of weapons, tossed there by Dutch soldiers as they fled from the Germans on the morning of May 10. There was even supposed to be a machine gun. They were going to try to salvage those weapons. That's all John had to know, said Father, and he had to keep as quiet as an Egyptian mummy about the whole affair.

John was the first to find a rifle. And then Father found one too. Uncle Gerrit took the weapons and hid them in the reeds. Whenever anyone passed by, they pretended that they were only out for a swim. Uncle Gerrit, sitting on the bank with his fishing pole, gave them the signal when it was safe for them to begin diving again.

Then John found the belts of ammunition for the machine gun. And close by, the machine gun itself. It was lodged in the mud so deeply that John couldn't bring it up by himself. But Uncle Gerrit was ready for anything. He took a coil of heavy cord from his tacklebox. John fastened it around the barrel of the machine gun and came up gasping for air. With all of them hauling, they managed to land the biggest catch of the day.

It was almost dark when Father and John got back home. Mother immediately herded them both to the bathroom, for they filled the house with the putrid stench of the canal. After dark, Uncle Gerrit also arrived, coming slowly across the fields with a wheelbarrow full of weapons. Father and Uncle Gerrit were busy for days cleaning them and packing them in grease. Then one day a truck came by and the weapons were hauled away underneath a load of potatoes. Neither John nor Father had any idea where they were going.

In the meantime, however, Father had told John more about the purpose of all this activity. A secret organization had been formed, a resistance movement, under the leadership of ex-officers mainly. It was called the O.D., and it was to go into action when it saw the

Germans were losing the war. Then its members would help drive out the enemy and at the same time stand ready to provide law and order in the vacuum left by the retreating Germans. For this they would need weapons, and they were already gathering and storing them in all parts of the country.

Later, Uncle Gerrit found out about another spot in the canal where rifles had been dumped. And one of Father's friends located a number of pistols. Uncle Gerrit was kept busy cleaning and polishing all these guns. But he loved it.

Then one day after the summer vacation had begun, a terrible thing happened! One morning, about 10 A.M., someone knocked hard on the front door. Margy was busy behind the house in the garden, and John was just coming downstairs, whistling to himself, so he opened the door. He looked up and stiffened with fear. Before him stood two German soldiers who barged past him into the house.

"Is Mr. De Boer home?" one of them barked in German. Without waiting for an answer, he clattered down the hall in his heavy boots and threw open the door to the family room. There was no one inside, so he banged open the next door down the hall. Father, standing behind his drawing board, looked up startled.

"Are you Mr. De Boer?" the officer demanded.

"Yes, I am," said Father calmly. "But I expected better manners from a German officer. Shouldn't you knock before entering someone's office? What can I do for you?"

John shuddered at Father's boldness. He didn't act at all afraid of the Germans. "I am here to place you under arrest," announced the German in an official tone. "Hands up!" snapped the other soldier, pointing his pistol at Father. He frisked Father but, of course, found nothing.

"Come along!" said the officer.

"Just a minute!" said Father. "What's this all about?"

"You'll see when we get downtown," Father was told. "Get your coat. Now!"

"Run and get Mother, John," Father said calmly, as he put on his coat.

John dashed into the garden. Behind the house stood another soldier, a rifle in his hands. Uncle Gerrit seemed to be making small talk with him. The man laughed loudly at one of the old man's jokes and slapped him on the back. Mother came hurrying toward the house, pale with fright.

"Don't be frightened, Mother," said John, as he intercepted her. "They're just taking Father downtown for questioning. It must be some mistake."

What he said, however, was only to put Mother at ease, for he himself was filled with dread. But he was still able to remain calm and think clearly. The cartoons? No, that was impossible. The songs? No, then they would have asked for him and not for Father. The weapons! There were still a few in the workshop! Half an hour ago Uncle Gerrit had been busy cleaning them at the workbench.

As Mother hurried into the house, John sauntered over toward the workshop, feigning nonchalance. The workbench was clear. Thank God!

When he returned to the house, Father was already being led out. Mother was conducting herself bravely and was trying to sway the German officer. But he only shrugged his shoulders. Father laughed. How could he? It even sounded quite natural.

"Don't worry, honey," he said to Mother, kissing her. "I'll be back soon. Take care of things, John. It's all a mix-up. It'll be straightened out soon, I'm sure."

A black car waited outside the gate. Father walked toward the car between the two German soldiers. Just as he was about to get in, Fritz came flying down the road on his bike. The bike crashed to the ground as Fritz leaped toward the two soldiers.

"Let go of my dad, you dirty Nazis!" he screamed, attacking the nearest man.

"Stop it, Fritz!" shouted Father.

The soldier gave Fritz a hard shove that sent him tumbling into the ditch. There he sat, sobbing wildly, as he watched the car carry Father away. Soon it was out of sight.

It was going to be a difficult day. They sat together around the kitchen table, worried and perplexed. In vain they asked themselves what it was all about. Uncle Gerrit had tried to sound out the soldier behind the house, but he had learned nothing. He was the only one whose outlook wasn't completely bleak. Or was he merely putting up a hopeful front?

"He wasn't picked up for any illegal business," he

maintained— and only John knew what he was referring to. "Otherwise, they would have searched the place. It has to be something else. But what? Still, no need to get into a stew over Everett. Just wait and see. Before you know it, he'll come back as free as a bird!"

"I surely hope and pray that you're right!" said Mother, sighing deeply.

John and Tricia never left Mother alone for very long during the day. In order to cheer her up, they hid their own anxiety and acted as if there was nothing to worry about.

John went to talk to Uncle Gerrit out in the garden.

"Did you hide those guns in a good place?" he asked. "Suppose those soldiers come back and . . . ."

"No need to bother your head about that," the old man assured him.

"Where did you put them?"

Uncle Gerrit squinted up at him as he knelt in the garden and said, "Just leave that to me. It's better if you don't know."

"Don't you trust me?" asked John.

"Like I trust myself," said Uncle Gerrit with a little smile. "But what you don't know can't hurt you. Don't *you* trust *me*?"

"Of course!" John answered.

"Then don't ask me where I put the guns. Instead, try to think. Has your father got anything else lying about the house?"

Then John mentioned the revolver that Father had taken along from Scheveningen. But Uncle Gerrit put his mind at ease. Father had already turned it over to

Van Vliet, he said.

Later, John remembered that there should be another cartoon somewhere, and he searched every corner of Father's studio. But he found nothing. Mother hadn't seen it either. That evening, when John was doing some more looking, the doorbell rang. He heard Margy opening the door, and he peered anxiously around the corner to see who it was. It was a stranger, and he insisted on seeing Mother. No, Margy couldn't take a message; he had to speak to Mother personally.

"Strange," thought John, "so late at night!" He hung around and kept his ears open.

The man handed Mother a note. "From your husband," he said. "He sends his love. Good night."

"May I ask your name?" Mother asked him.

"You're better off not knowing," he said. He tipped his cap and strode back to his bicycle.

The note really was from Father. It was a page torn from his date book, and it was covered with his neat script.

"Dear wife," it said. "I was right. It is a mistake! I have been charged with striking down a German soldier on May 10, when he tried to commandeer our car. I don't know where they got such a fantastic idea! They have no proof whatsoever. But they don't want to believe me. It's all Schram's doing. He's part of the S.D. here. Keep faith! Everything will be straightened out. Everett John."

Mother read the note first, and John read along over her shoulder. But then Tricia and Fritz had to hear it too, of course. Fritz jumped up out of his chair after

Mother finished reading the letter aloud.

"Then I did see him!" he exclaimed. "He rode by here on his bike a while ago, but I couldn't believe it was him. He looked so different in his uniform. The dirty traitor! That rabbit-faced coward!"

Suddenly he began to sob. "It's my fault! It's my fault Dad's in jail! If only I hadn't told that crazy story of yours." Through his tears he glared accusingly at Tricia.

Mother put Fritz to bed early. John and Tricia sat at the table together. They didn't sob like Fritz, but they felt like it. When Father had scolded Fritz in Scheveningen for spreading his story, Fritz had got the idea that Tricia had made it all up. But John and Tricia knew better.

They sat up awhile with Mother in the half-darkened room. Suddenly they were filled with fear. It was no mistake! Father had written the way he did just in case the note fell into the wrong hands. Did they really have no proof? What if the paratrooper appeared personally to accuse Father? But that didn't seem likely. All German prisoners had been immediately shipped to England during the war. "No proof whatsoever," Father had written. But what if they had found the rifle . . . or the helmet?

None of them could do a thing, however. All they could do was wait and see. They pondered and considered all the possibilities. And they prayed! Which was no little thing—that they were sure of. Prayer gave them a bond with Father as he sat in jail. They entrusted him to God's keeping. For God alone could save him from the enemy and bring him safely back to them.

CHAPTER TWELVE

The next day about 9 o'clock, Fritz was pedaling through town toward the prison. When he got there, he circled it once, staring up at the barred windows. Behind one of those windows was his Father. But which one?

Last night he hadn't been able to get to sleep—until suddenly a plan had formed in his mind. Once the plan was complete, he had drifted off and had slept until 7 o'clock. After breakfast, he had secretly taken his bike and slipped away. Now he was ready to carry out his design. He didn't hesitate. Fritz wasn't frightened very easily, and he had never been bothered with bashfulness. His only fear was that his plan might fail. But now it was up to him. If he didn't succeed, it wasn't going to be for want of trying!

He stopped at the front door of the prison, parked his bike, and rang the bell. A few minutes later a small hatch opened in the door, and the face of a guard peered out at Fritz.

"What do you want, kid?" he demanded.

"I've got to speak to the director," said Fritz. "Right now!"

"Oh, you do, do you? Listen, kid! We don't have time for nonsense around here. And not for lippy young brats either. So beat it! You can't see the director!" And he slammed the hatch closed.

But if he thought he could get rid of Fritz so easily, he was mistaken. Fritz rang again—long and loud. This time the hatch popped open right away.

"Didn't you hear me, kid?" the guard snapped, really angry now.

"Didn't you hear *me*?" Fritz answered fearlessly. "I've *got* to speak to the director right now! I have an important message for him."

"What about?" asked the guard, beginning to hesitate.

"I can't tell you," said Fritz. "But you can bet he'll be mad at you if he finds out you sent me away. I'll call him up and tell on you. I'll tell him it was the man at the door with the red face, and then he'll know who you are!"

The hatch closed for the second time. But this time he heard the rattle of keys and the sound of a lock being turned. Then the door swung open. Fritz immediately stepped inside. The door closed behind him, and the lock clicked again.

They stood in a kind of foyer that was divided from the hallway beyond by a gate of steel bars. The guard walked over to the gate, rattling his keys, and unlocked it for Fritz.

"What's your name?" he asked, as he let Fritz through.

"Fritz De Boer," said Fritz, very dignified.

He had to wait a while as the guard took his time about closing and locking the gate again.

"Wait here," said the man, and he knocked on a nearby door with a window in it. Inside the room, Fritz could see a bald-headed man with a little beard. He was sitting at a desk writing. He exchanged a few words with the guard. Then a puzzled look appeared on his face, and he shrugged his shoulders. But Fritz ended up being escorted into the room anyway.

"What is it, my boy?" the man asked. And Fritz sensed immediately that this was a kind person.

"They put my father in this jail, sir," he said. "And it's all my fault. And I've come to ask you to please let him go."

"I see . . . I see," said the man nodding gravely, but Fritz could see the wrinkles of laughter about his eyes. "And who is your father?"

"My father is the best architect in the whole country," said Fritz. "He can make the most beautiful houses you've ever seen!"

"Really!" added Fritz, a little miffed when he saw the man starting to smile. He had to believe that Fritz was telling the truth.

"Yes, I see. But what's his *name*?"

"Oh! His name is De Boer, just like me. Everett John De Boer."

"I see . . . I see," said the bald-headed man again. He

seemed to see a lot. "So you're Everett John's little boy. And why is it your fault that your daddy is in jail?"

"I'd better explain it very carefully," thought Fritz; "otherwise this old man won't understand."

He began, "Well, you see. When we were in Scheveningen, I was bragging about my dad to the kids on the block, you know. But it wasn't true at all, don't you see? And then that dirty . . . I mean that . . . ."

The door behind Fritz was thrown open, and in marched a German officer. The officer flung out his arm and shouted, "Heil Hitler!" Fritz saw the kind face of the bald-headed old man suddenly grow hard and withdrawn, but he saluted back.

Then the officer saw Fritz and exclaimed in German, "Hey! What on earth are you doing here?"

Fritz didn't understand, but the old man talked to the officer in German, and then Fritz had to tell his story from the beginning once more. Fritz guessed that this must be one of the Germans that had picked up Father yesterday, and a sudden surge of hope rose in his chest. He had to explain slowly, sentence by sentence, while the old man translated into German.

"Why did you tell this strange story?" the German asked through the old man.

"Well," said Fritz. "Those kids were saying that my dad was scared. Just because my dad was *smarter* than the other dads on the block! Right away he said that we were going to lose the war. So the other kids said he was chicken!"

"How did you come up with such a story? Did you think it up all by yourself?"

"Yessir!" said Fritz, nodding. He could hardly tattle on Tricia. They might put her in jail. Then she would cry night and day. "Yessiree, I thought it up all by myself, because the kids said . . . ."

"Yes, yes! I know. But did you perhaps hear a story like that from someone else?"

"No, sir. But people were saying that German soldiers were taking people's cars. And then I thought, if they tried to take *our* car, then my dad would show them! And then I made up a story so that those kids would stop saying nasty things about my dad. And now my dad is getting punished for it, and that isn't fair! But you'll let him out, won't you?"

Fritz turned to the German officer, for he had quickly caught on that he was the real boss around there. "You won't keep my dad in jail now, will you, sir?"

"But then *you'll* have to take his place," said the German, and Fritz understood even before the old man could translate.

"Okay," he said, nodding. That was all right with him. They wouldn't keep him for long, anyway. Even the German was starting to look friendly. He put his hand on Fritz's head.

"You're a bold little rascal!" he said. Fritz nodded, his eyes downcast in shame. The hand on his head lingered there a moment and ruffled his hair. Fritz forced himself not to flinch. "Let him pat your head all he wants," he told himself. "As long as he lets Dad out of jail!" He would purr like a kitten and lick the German's hand if he would set Dad free.

The German officer took the bald-headed old man

aside and whispered to him. The old man, in turn, called a guard into the office.

"Get number forty-seven," he said.

The guard disappeared down the hall, and Fritz was told to sit on a sofa and wait. The German lit up a cigarette and studied Fritz with a kindly smile.

"It worked," Fritz thought. "My plan worked!" He sat fidgeting on the edge of the sofa.

There were footsteps in the hall. The door opened. Sure enough!

"Dad!" cried Fritz, and he threw himself into Father's arms.

"Fritz!" cried Father, in surprise. "What are you doing here?"

The German officer began to explain to Father. Fritz kept his eyes fixed on the German's mouth. Although he couldn't understand what the man was saying, he was sure that everything was going to be all right. Everything had been straightened out. Fritz's story agreed with Father's explanation.

"My apologies, sir," said the German, and he even bowed to Father!

And then he ruffled Fritz's hair again. "I've got a boy like him at home too—a dear little scamp just like him." And he took Fritz's face between his hands and looked into his eyes with a wistful smile.

Father got his watch back and his wallet and several other things. They had even taken away his belt. Then they were ready to go. Fritz had to shake hands with the German officer. The man said something, and he laughed at his own remark. So Fritz laughed too, even though he hadn't understood a word of it. And then the German wanted to shake his hand again. Fritz was beginning to get fed up with the man's fawning over him. Still, he had freed Father! For that he was even willing to kiss the man, if necessary. Soon he would be home with Father!

When they were finally on their way down the hall, they heard the German say, "Bring that Schram in here!" and his voice no longer sounded friendly.

It was still morning when Father and Fritz came walking through the front gate. Fritz was walking his bike. The rest of the family came hurtling out of the front door, almost running each other down. Even old Uncle Gerrit with his crooked old legs came running from behind the house. Fritz was beaming. Everyone hugged him and was amazed at his daring. He had walked right into the lion's den.

"I'd still be sitting in my cell if he hadn't come!" said Father.

It became a big party. Tricia fetched special treats from the bakery and Mother made lemonade and coffee. Uncle Gerrit got some big cigars from somewhere, and he and Father sat back blowing smoke rings.

"Can I have a puff?" asked Fritz.

Of course, he could! He was the hero of the day! But Fritz got tears in his eyes and coughed till he was out of breath. He couldn't see what was so special about cigars, he said. Mother gave him an extra pastry, and that was more to his liking. John gave him his air rifle and Tricia shoved her new detective novel into his hands. Uncle Gerrit promised to show him how to carve a flute out of a willow branch. Everyone spoiled Fritz outrageously. But to have Mother and Father sitting among them side by side, smiling at each other, was no small gift. And it had all been Fritz's doing!

After dinner, when Father and John were in the studio by themselves, John asked, "Dad, where did you put that cartoon that was left? I turned the whole place upside down looking for it, but I couldn't find it anywhere!"

Father slid a couple of books out of the bookcase and reached behind. Carefully he pried a brick out of the wall and stuck his hand in the hole.

"Here it is," said Father. "You think anyone would have found it there?"

John studied the cartoon once more: "Our New Daddy." It was perfect! The skinny little squealer looked almost like Schram. But they would get the fat officer out of that chair. With men like the little kid sneaking up on the German, like Fritz . . . John sighed. He wanted to keep the cartoon, but it was too dangerous.

"Shouldn't we burn it, Father?" he asked.

"Nope!" said Father. "We're not going to let them scare us so easily, are we, John? This is a war not between nations or people, first of all. But between different principles. Between good and evil. Between God and satan. At least, that's how I see it.

The Nazis have invaded our country, and now they're

trying to win the people. They're trying to poison our hearts with their evil doctrines. But it won't work, John! And we'll help to see that it doesn't. We'll have to be very careful, of course. We've had our first warning. But we won't give up until—with God's help—the Nazi night will turn to day.

"Remember what Uncle Gerrit said when the war first started, John? Things may look dark now, but with God there's always light at the end of the tunnel."

John looked at the cartoon once more. Then he carefully put it back in the hole in the wall.

APPENDIX

When early on the morning of May 10, 1940, the German ambassador to the Netherlands delivered a declaration of war to the Dutch government in The Hague, German troops had been crossing the border for several hours, and German planes were already attacking The Hague. The pretext for Germany's invasion of the Netherlands was that the latter was a partner in an Anglo-French plot to invade Germany through Belgium, Luxembourg, and the Netherlands.

In its concerted air attack on all major Dutch airfields, Germany virtually wiped out the small Dutch air force. Thereafter, the *Luftwaffe* virtually had its own way in the air. Most Dutch planes were destroyed on the ground by the bombing, and others were shot up by German parachute troops. Hundreds of parachutists were being dropped around strategic centers in the heart of Holland at the same time that the borders were being crossed. The Hague, the seat of government; Rotterdam; and Amsterdam, the capital, were the primary targets.

These parachute troops caused destruction far beyond their numbers. Some were disguised as Dutch soldiers or civilians; in The Hague and Rotterdam, they were assisted by Germans living in Holland and by Dutch Nazis. These forces not only spread fears, rumors, and near panic in these areas, but also tied up large numbers of troops. They were kept busy searching for German paratroopers and hence could not serve as reserves for the front lines.

Knowing that they couldn't possibly hold the long border that they shared with Germany against the latter's vastly superior military might, the Dutch conceived a strategy that was meant to delay the advance of German troops as long as possible in order to allow for the arrival of Allied support. The Dutch had mobilised several times already in response to false reports of a German invasion, and they had already flooded some areas to impede a German advance.

The German troops that swept into the northern part of the Netherlands (Groningen, Friesland, and Drenthe) met little resistance until they got close to the Outer Dike, which separates Lake Yssel (or the Zuider Zee) from the Wadden Sea. After strong resistance, Wons fell to heavy air and artillery attacks. But the Dutch were better fortified at Kornwerderzand, right on the big dike, and could not be dislodged.

Further south, Dutch troops were able to keep the Germans from crossing the border for a while, and then, after flooding large areas and blowing up bridges, they pulled back to the Yssel Line, namely, the Yssel River, which had been fortified on its west bank. The next line of defense to which the central western divisions retreated was the Grebbe Line, which followed the valley that extends from the bottom of Lake Yssel through Amersfoort to the Meuse River. Here, too, water defenses created by flooding played an important role.

The southern end of this line was extended almost straight south through North Brabant by the Dutch troops which had been forced to abandon the southeast corner of the Netherlands. Some of these troops also retreated across Belgium and joined French and Dutch troops in Zeeland, where they continued fighting several days after the rest of the country had surrendered.

Meanwhile, German parachutists had seized the airfields of Ypenburg, Ockenburg, and Valkenburg around The Hague. Their objective was to capture Queen Wilhelmina and her government. The parachute troops that landed in the vicinity of Rotterdam and Dordrecht, aided by Germans living in Rotterdam and by Dutch Nazis managed to seize intact several bridges at Moerdyk. This was the main traffic artery between the northern and southern parts of the country.

The strategic air base at Waalhaven, south of Rotterdam, also fell into German hands. With these airfields in their possession, the Germans could fly in more reinforcements. However, the Dutch soon recaptured all three airfields around The Hague and squashed all German activity in the area. But German troops at Moerdyk and Waalhaven were solidly entrenched in their positions and could not be dislodged, despite some fierce fighting.

The last line of defense after the Grebbe Line was the well-fortified "Fortress of Holland," designed to protect the rich urban centers of the nation. But by seizing the bridges at Moerdyk, the Germans had a way across the natural defense formed by the Meuse (or Maas) River. The German attack on the Dutch positions in the southern part of the country (in North Brabant) was the most successful of all; and, soon, German troops were heading for Moerdyk and Rotterdam to join with the parachute troops there and thus breach the imposing "Fortress of Holland."

On the fourth day of fighting, General H.G. Winkelman, the Dutch Commander in Chief, advised the Queen and the members of the Dutch parliament that he could no longer guarantee their safety, so a government-in-exile was set up in London. Queen Wilhelmina herself later went on to Canada and spent the duration of the war in Ottawa. In effect, this put General Winkelman in charge of the country.

Although the Dutch defensive position was not hopeless, the German threat to bomb all major Dutch cities, starting with Rotterdam and Utrecht, forced Winkelman to consider surrender. The Germans ruled the sky, so this was no weak threat. Moreover, by this time Winkelman had learned that the expected help from the Allies was not coming. So defeat was only a matter of time, and further resistance could be very costly.

Therefore, Winkelman agreed to negotiate a surrender. During the negotiations German bombers made repeated attacks on the heart of Rotterdam, reducing it to ashes and killing hundreds of civilians. Winkelman immediately ordered his men to surrender.

It was the end of a short war and the beginning of a long occupation. For most people in the Netherlands, the struggle was just beginning.

NORTH SEA

WADDEN SEA

GRONINGEN
Delfzijl
Leeuwarden • Groningen • Harlingen
Kornwerderzand Wons FRIESLAND
Outer Dike Assen
DRENTHE
NORTH Meppel
HOLLAND LAKE YSSEL
Kampen
Zwolle Ommen
Haarlem Hatten OVERYSSEL
Amsterdam Yssel R. Deventer
Leiden Amersfoort Apeldoorn
Scheveningen The Hague Utrecht GELDER-LAND
Ockenburg Ypenburg UTRECHT Arnhem
Hook of Delft Upper Rhine R.
Holland Rotterdam
Waalhaven Dordrecht Waal R. Nymegen
Meuse R. Rhine R.
Moerdyk Vught
ZEELAND Breda NORTH
Middelburg Tilburg Duisburg Essen
Zeeland- BRABANT
Flanders Eindhoven Düsseldorf
Antwerp LIMBURG

Ghent

BELGIUM

Brussels Maastricht Cologne

GERMANY